Everybody loved Josh Cooper.

Including Toni Marsh. But Toni didn't just love the public face. She knew the hidden aspects of Josh's character. The soft spot for children which he would vociferously deny if challenged. The sadness when he couldn't help a patient any further. Even the bad temper directed at her in the wake of a hangover. She knew more of the real Josh Cooper than anyone did. And she loved every part of him.

Alison Roberts was born in New Zealand and she says, 'I lived in London and Washington D.C. as a child and began my working career as a primary-school teacher. A lifelong interest in medicine was fostered by my doctor and nurse parents, flatting with doctors and physiotherapists on leaving home, and marriage to a house surgeon who is now a consultant cardiologist. I have also worked as a cardiology technician and research assistant. My husband's medical career took us to Glasgow for two years, which was an ideal place and time to start my writing career. I now live in Christchurch, New Zealand, with my husband, daughter, and various pets.'

Recent titles by the same author:

AN IRRESISTIBLE ATTRACTION
DEFINITELY DADDY
A CHANGE OF HEART
PERFECT TIMING

A PERFECT RESULT

BY
ALISON ROBERTS

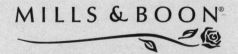

MILLS & BOON®

MILLS & BOON and MILLS & BOON with the Rose Device are registered trademarks of the publisher.

First published in Great Britain 2000
Harlequin Mills & Boon Limited,
Eton House, 18-24 Paradise Road, Richmond, Surrey TW9 1SR

© Alison Roberts 2000

ISBN 0 263 82265 6

Set in Times Roman 10½ on 12 pt.
03-0010-45115

Printed and bound in Spain
by Litografía Rosés, S.A., Barcelona

CHAPTER ONE

IT WAS a perfect day for a wedding.

The small stone church was surrounded with a sea of golden daffodils, nodding happily in the gentle nor'-westerly breeze. The sky was a perfect, clear blue. The low covering of snow on the Southern Alps away to the west declared the ski season to be far from over, but as usual August in Canterbury, New Zealand, was giving a definite hint of better things to come. A promise of renewal. A new beginning. Hope.

Toni Marsh closed her eyes for a second, concentrating on the well rehearsed tones of the minister's voice.

'Dearly beloved, we are gathered here together in the sight of God, and in the presence of this congregation, to join together this man and this woman...'

Toni could feel the magic of the ceremony, the beauty of a public declaration of love and commitment. She knew exactly how Sophie Bennett must be feeling, especially when Oliver Spencer's voice caught with emotion as he repeated his vows, knowing that in a moment she would have the chance to declare her own devotion to him. Till death parted them.

It touched a deep chord within Toni. She didn't care what the statistics said. Some people *were* capable of finding the right person, were faithful and loyal and giving enough to make it last. To grow. To become something that could never be demeaned by statistics or written off as an outdated institution. Some people still believed in marriage. Like Sophie and Oliver.

Like Toni.

'…in sickness and in health, to love, honour and cherish, till death us do part.'

Toni's gaze dropped to the bouquet she held. The tiny jonquils nestled amongst the miniature white roses and gypsophila. This was the first time she had stood at the front of a church as a member of a wedding party. Separate from the congregation. Close to the minister. She could almost imagine it was her own wedding. If someone waved a wand and made Sophie and Oliver vanish then she would be standing there…with Dr Josh Cooper.

'Could I have the rings, please?' The minister nodded at the best man.

Josh felt inside the left pocket of his suit jacket. Then he tried the right pocket. His eyes widened in consternation. Toni felt a flicker of alarm but then saw the grin Josh couldn't quite suppress. He produced the ring box from his inside breast pocket. Oliver and Sophie exchanged amused glances but Toni gave Josh a disapproving glance.

It was typical of Josh Cooper to do something to try and defuse an emotionally charged situation. Anything heavy simply had to be lightened. It was a wonder Oliver had managed to talk him into being best man at all. Josh's horror at the prospect of marriage had been continually reinforced over the years Toni had known him. Any mention of the 'M' word ensured that the guilty woman received an even shorter than usual inclusion in Josh Cooper's social agenda.

'I now pronounce you husband and wife,' the minister said with relish. He smiled benevolently. 'You may kiss the bride.'

Toni saw the expression on Oliver's face as he adjusted Sophie's veil, and her breath caught. She would settle for a look like that being bestowed on her, just once in her lifetime, and she would feel it had all been worthwhile. Tears, which hadn't been far away for the whole ceremony, prickled ominously. Toni blinked furiously and hoped that her mascara was waterproof. It had been so long since she'd worn any it hadn't occurred to her to ask. It had been Sophie's idea to take advantage of the make-up expert available at the hairdressing salon. The occasion had already been enough to encourage Toni to make some serious changes to her appearance. What was one more, after all?

The collective sigh of satisfaction from the congregation as the kiss became prolonged made Toni smile. The threat of smudged mascara receded and she glanced at Josh to see if he was also enjoying the enthusiasm the bridal couple were displaying. But Josh wasn't watching Oliver and Sophie. He was staring at Toni, a puzzled frown creasing his forehead.

He moved to stand beside her as Oliver and Sophie went to sign the register.

'You look...different,' he said accusingly. His brown eyes raked her face.

'Do I?' Toni's pulse jumped. How different? she wondered. Different enough to change his opinion of her? Different enough to promote her from long-time reliable employee, dogsbody and long-suffering repair technician for any personal or professional hassles? Different enough to be of interest as a woman? 'Must

be the dress,' she said lightly. 'You've never seen me
dressed up before.'

'Hmm.' Josh's gaze travelled down her slim figure,
outlined by the elegant, jonquil yellow silk sheath. He
smiled thoughtfully and nodded. 'You scrub up rather
nicely, Swampy.'

'Thanks.' Toni's tone was dry. Did he have any
idea at all how much she loathed the nickname?
Probably not. It had never occurred to Toni to complain because it was always delivered affectionately—
one of the few treasured indications that Josh Cooper
was fond of his practice manager. A sign that she was
special enough to be given a name only he used. It
was only recently that it had started to rankle. The
name made her think of dark, damp, boggy places.
Undesirable. Like her.

The garden surrounding the little church was a little
damp and boggy underfoot but nobody was complain-
ing. The gnarled trunks of the venerable oak trees
with the carpet of bluebells was a wedding photographer's dream. He arranged the wedding party and
began taking pictures.

'Is my lipstick OK?' Sophie asked Toni anxiously.

'Tasted fine to me,' Oliver declared.

'That's what I'm worried about.' Sophie grinned.
'I think you ate it all.'

'Looks fine,' Toni assured her. She reached out to
tuck the veil further back from Sophie's face. 'Shame
to hide that gorgeous hairdo,' she murmured. The
bride's shoulder-length, straight hair had been drawn
up into an intricate knot, dotted with tiny white flowers. Tendrils had been left and curled into ringlets that
framed her face.

'At least we can see yours.' Sophie smiled. 'It looks stunning, Toni.'

'I like it, too,' Toni agreed shyly. 'I would never have had the courage to make such a major change if it hadn't been for your hairdresser.'

'*That's* what it is,' Josh announced triumphantly. 'I knew there was something different about you. You've got your hair loose.'

Toni and Sophie exchanged smiles.

'Men!' Sophie clucked happily. She linked her arm with Oliver's and beamed at the photographer. 'You're all hopeless.' It was clearly too much to expect Josh to notice that the length of Toni's hair was shorter by at least twelve inches. Now it was only slightly longer than Sophie's and the layering had released waves Toni had been unaware of possessing.

'It's not just the hair, though, is it?' Josh ignored the photographer's plea to look straight ahead at the camera. He was still staring at Toni. 'There's something else.'

'Spell it out for him, Toni,' Oliver advised, 'otherwise we'll never get through.'

'I'm not wearing my glasses,' Toni told Josh. 'I don't need them any more.'

Josh was silent, clearly disconcerted that he hadn't noticed something so obvious. Toni felt sorry for him. She knew how different she looked. It had been an astonishing revelation, looking in the mirror as she and Sophie had made the final preparations for the wedding. It reminded her of those classic movie scenes where the secretary ripped off her spectacles and loosed the tightly scraped-back long hair, transforming herself from boring to voluptuous in one fell swoop.

Toni's swoop had taken a little longer. It had been three months since she'd begun the process of laser surgery to cure her short-sightedness, but it was only in the last couple of days that the spectacles had finally gone, no longer needed even to hold the post-surgical padding in place. Her face felt curiously naked without them. Vulnerable. Especially under the intense scrutiny Josh was subjecting her to. He didn't look as though her transformation had unleashed any secret passion, however. Toni sighed lightly before she smiled at the photographer again. Josh looked vaguely worried—as though the change in her appearance might herald a similar disruption to her professional capabilities.

The photographer took a series of pictures of the bride and groom, before calling for the best man and bridesmaid. Toni felt conspicuous, standing alone with Josh. She smiled a trifle grimly, keeping her line of vision focused on a scene well behind the camera.

St David's practice nurse, Janet Muir, was standing beside the minister. She was clearly giving her twin sons a good telling-off. The minister also looked disapprovingly down at the small boys who stood, temporarily repentant, with bunches of illicitly plucked daffodils in their fists. Toni's mouth twitched into a much more genuine smile and she complied with the photographer's request without hesitation, moving closer to Josh and linking their arms.

'A bit gruesome, isn't it?' Josh murmured. He glanced down at Toni with a twisted smile. 'Do you know, I broke out in a cold sweat during that ceremony? I could almost imagine it was *me* tying the knot.'

'Too close for comfort, was it?' Toni caught Josh's

eye as she looked up quizzically. She searched his face briefly, wondering if Josh had really been protesting too much over the years and whether his real opinion of marriage was something quite different to his advertised beliefs. The swift grin she received put an end to that line of thought.

'You know me so well, Swampy. I won't be doing this again. For anyone!'

She did know him so well. Josh live-life-to-the-full Cooper. Too fond of fast cars and fast women. Too interested in hedonistic pursuits, like drinking fine wine, sampling gourmet food, dancing and the adrenaline rush of dangerous recreational activities. Josh of the catch phrases 'life's too short' and 'just go for it'. Josh who could never take anything personal very seriously. Toni had to admit he seemed to be taking his duties as master of ceremonies today quite seriously, however. The move to the reception venue had been smooth and the entertainment and refreshment of the gathering continued without a hitch.

The wedding party was supposed to be seated at the head table while the guests helped themselves from the hot buffet. Despite the temptation of the excellent food being served, Toni found her partner wasn't present at the small table for more than a few minutes at a time. Josh was circulating amongst the guests, competing with waiters to top up champagne flutes, escorting Oliver's great-aunt Agnes to the buffet and discussing the merits of every morsel he placed on her plate, pausing to chat for a moment to everyone who managed to catch his eye.

The tailored jacket of his formal, dark grey suit had been discarded, the sleeves of the silk dress shirt pushed up, the grey waistcoat unbuttoned, but Josh still managed to look more elegant than any other man present. Toni's gaze was still following him, her dessert abandoned, when Janet dropped into the empty seat on her right.

'You look stunning, Toni. I almost didn't recognise you when you came into the church.'

'Thanks, Jan. I'm not sure I recognise myself.' Toni smiled at her colleague. 'I love your dress—perfect colour for you.'

Janet Muir's dress was a deep shade of delphinium blue, just a shade darker than her eyes. A matching headband was valiantly attempting to subdue the exuberant curls of her auburn hair. She grinned at Toni.

'I just hope it stays together till I get home. I didn't finish making it until two o'clock this morning. The hemming was more than a wee bit sloppy.' Janet's brow creased anxiously. 'Have you seen the twins recently?'

'Mmm.' Toni suppressed a smile. 'They were picking the icing flowers off the wedding cake.'

'Oh, no!' Janet gasped. 'The little horrors. They *promised* to behave themselves.' She began to rise to her feet but Toni patted her hand.

'Don't worry. Josh sorted them out. Look.' Toni pointed towards the guests' tables. Josh had a small boy on either side of him. Two curly blond heads were bent, seriously intent on their tasks. Both boys had white cloths draped over the arms of their matching denim jackets. They each held a bottle of champagne.

'Uh-oh!' Janet murmured. 'Not a good idea, Josh.'

But the boys were managing well. Josh supported the base of the bottles discreetly as first Adam and then Rory charmed guests by topping up glasses and then beaming proudly at their achievements. Some form of non-verbal communication had two waiters replacing Josh's supervision a minute later and Janet ducked back to her own table as he returned. Josh tapped his knife on his glass to gain everyone's attention and then waited for silence.

'According to Billy Connolly, marriage is a wonderful invention but, then again, so is a bicycle repair kit.' Josh waited for the laughter to subside. 'Personally I haven't needed either yet, but seeing Oliver and Sophie together today I'm inclined to agree more with Samuel Johnson who described marriage as ''the triumph of hope over experience''. If my own experience of a partnership with Oliver Spencer is anything to go by, the hope is very well placed.'

The murmur of approval from Josh's audience made Toni glance away. Oliver and Sophie were gazing at each other and were holding hands. Josh stood beside them, a glass held casually in his hand, the centre of attention as he told the guests of the beginning of his partnership with Oliver some four years ago.

Four years. It seemed like yesterday. Josh was making it sound as if Oliver had rescued St David's and turned it into the flourishing medical centre it was today, but Toni knew better than that. Better than anybody. Her own association with St David's—and Josh—went back nearly ten years. Josh had been twenty-eight, an enthusiastic young doctor buying his first general practice from the finally retiring Dr Jamieson. It had been well past time for the old doctor to bow out. St David's patient numbers had been declining steadily for years as locals grew weary of the slow pace and old-fashioned methods Dr Jamieson had clung to.

The practice hadn't changed overnight. It had taken nearly three years for Josh to build patient numbers up to a level that ensured financial viability for the practice. Toni had willingly helped in whatever capacity she could, often working over the part time hours she'd been paid for. She'd been proud of the reputation Josh had garnered, evidenced by the ever-increasing patient base.

She'd shared his excitement when he'd taken on Oliver Spencer as a junior partner and shortly afterwards had employed Janet Muir as St David's practice nurse. Her own pride in being promoted to practice manager and full time employment hadn't faded either. They were a close team, now with the welcome addition of Sophie. Toni smiled at the youngest member of the team at the same time Josh did.

'Sophie came to us at the beginning of this year as a GP registrar,' Josh informed the wedding guests, as he continued the speech Toni had only been half listening to. 'Oliver was happy to act as her supervisor and tutor. I did sometimes wonder what was being taught in those tutorial sessions.' Josh waited for the amusement to subside yet again. The audience had thoroughly enjoyed his account of several embarrassing incidents of his professional association with Oliver. They were relaxed, ready to turn their attention to the bride and the toast they all knew Josh was leading up to.

'We knew Sophie was planning a wedding,' Josh continued. A few looks were exchanged amongst the guests and Sophie blushed. Her long-standing engagement on her arrival at St David's had been common knowledge. Toni thought of the stack of her treasured magazines containing wedding articles which she'd loaned to Sophie and which had been left to gather dust under the young doctor's desk.

'We were just getting used to the idea that Sophie might have changed her mind when we discovered that Oliver was also planning a wedding.' Josh nodded slowly. 'It all made perfect sense only when we discovered—to our delight—that they were planning to marry each other. And now they have.'

Josh paused for a long moment. The guests smiled in anticipation of the joke they knew had to come, a finishing touch which only Josh Cooper would have the nerve to produce. Even Sophie and Oliver were waiting with expressions of amused resignation. But the best man's face stilled and his smile faded.

'The American Indians have a marriage ceremony which includes these lines.' Josh seemed to take a deep breath as he turned an unusually solemn gaze onto the bridal couple.

'Now you will feel no rain, for each of you will be shelter for the other.

Now you will feel no cold, for each of you will be warmth to the other.

Now there is no more loneliness.

Now you are two persons but there is only one life before you.'

Josh raised his glass. The absolute silence was broken by his quiet toast. 'To Oliver and Sophie.'

Toni reached for her own glass but found the words she should repeat caught in her throat. She felt ridiculously close to tears again and she saw several guests reach for tissues as well as their glasses. The cutting of the cake passed in a blur. How could Josh have come up with something so beautiful? And so serious. Or was it just that the impact had been so much greater because of its unexpectedness?

As if to make up for his emotional lapse, Josh seemed to have moved into a higher gear. He was amongst the crowd again, serving cake and laughingly coping with the open adoration Oliver's young female cousins were bestowing on him.

And why not? Toni finished her glass of champagne with a gulp. Josh had to be the star attraction for any single female present. He was a highly respected doctor. Josh might squeeze every ounce of enjoyment out of his own time but his life was clearly divided between work and play. His work was too brilliant for anything in his private life—including his reputation for playing the field—to count against him.

Josh was also good-looking, eligible and confident. He was caring, funny and game for anything. Everybody loved Josh Cooper. Including Toni Marsh. But Toni didn't just love the public face. She knew the hidden aspects of Josh's character. The soft spot for children which he would vociferously deny if challenged. The sadness when he couldn't help a patient any further. Even the bad temper directed at her in the wake of a hangover. She knew more of the real Josh Cooper than anyone did. And she loved every part of him.

The tables were cleared and moved as Janet Muir gathered up her sons and excused herself.

'I'd love to stay for the dancing,' she told Toni wistfully, 'but I'll have to get these two home. Make sure you catch the bouquet later!'

'If I do, I'll give it to you,' Toni said with a smile. 'I think it's a bit late for me.'

'It's definitely a bit late for these boys.' Janet smiled as she ruffled the curls of her tired twins. 'Oh, look—there are Sophie and Oliver, dancing. Don't they look lovely?'

Adam and Rory yawned and Janet shook her head. 'Come on. Home to bed.' Josh materialised beside Toni as she watched the door close behind Janet. Josh caught Toni's hand and gave her an encouraging tug. 'It's our duty to dance,' he told her. 'It's the signal for everyone to join in. I read it in my *How To Be A Best Man* guide.'

Toni tried to suppress the disappointment she felt. Would Josh have asked her to dance at all if it hadn't been one of his official duties? The feeling left as soon as she found herself in his arms, however. As soon as she felt the touch of his hands through the silky fabric covering her back.

It was by no means an unfamiliar sensation. Josh often touched her at work—a quick squeeze of her shoulder as he went past, a pat of gratitude for some task completed. Even a hug on her birthday or similarly appropriate occasion. It always had the same effect, and right now it was magnified unbearably by the romantic waltz in which Josh was guiding her.

It was like being offered a glass of the most desirable wine in existence. Having the glass touch your lips so that you were able to smell it and almost taste it. Close enough to know that once you tasted it you would never want to try another wine ever again. And then to have the glass removed, just before the liquid touched your lips.

Josh held her as though he could sense her emotional turmoil. He gazed down at Toni with gentle sympathy.

'Weddings make you go all mushy, don't they? You really believe in the plighting of troths for better or worse and so on.'

'Yes, I do,' Toni confirmed softly. 'Till death us do part.'

Josh's hold became stiff. The rhythm of the dance was marred. Toni could feel his tension and cursed herself for saying the wrong thing. Other couples were now drifting onto the dance floor. Toni could sense Josh looking over her shoulder, his attention now focused elsewhere.

'Do you think we've done enough of our formal duties?' Josh sounded a little embarrassed. 'It's just that I've promised Oliver's cousins a turn each out here and there are a few to get through. It wouldn't do to disappoint any of them.'

'Oh, we couldn't have that,' Toni agreed lightly. 'It wouldn't do your reputation any good at all.' She stepped quickly out of his arms. 'I've had enough of dancing for the moment anyway. These shoes are killing my feet.'

Toni found herself sitting alone at the table. She picked up her glass of champagne only to find it empty. A waiter was cruising nearby with a bottle and he glanced in Toni's direction. She looked away. Drinking too much was no solution to anything.

The music changed. The loud rock and roll number brought a whoop of delight from Josh. His enthusiasm rippled through the crowd and the tempo picked up instantly.

'Hopeless.' Toni shook her head wearily but she smiled at the same time. 'Let the party begin!' She held up her empty glass to signal the waiter.

'What the hell,' she said aloud.

It wasn't Josh Cooper who was hopeless. It was herself. Hopelessly in love with someone who didn't know. And wouldn't want to know.

CHAPTER TWO

THERE was still no sign of him.

Ten past nine and Mrs Bradshaw was sighing heavily as she flicked the pages of her magazine. Toni glanced anxiously at the clock as she reached for the phone.

'St David's Medical Centre. Toni speaking.' She listened, reaching for her pencil. 'I'm sorry but Dr Spencer will be away all week, Mr Campbell. He's on his honeymoon.' She listened again. 'I'm afraid Dr Cooper is fully booked for today. We will have a locum available this afternoon. Is it urgent?' Toni flipped over pages in the appointment book. 'Well, how about we make it next Tuesday? Ten a.m.?'

Filling in the slot, Toni looked up as the front door opened. It wasn't Josh. A woman carrying her baby in a car seat smiled at Toni.

'Hi. I've brought Melissa in for her six-week check.'

Toni couldn't help leaning over the counter to admire the sleeping infant. 'Oh, she's gorgeous, Jenny. How's everything going?'

'Apart from not getting much sleep, it's fine.'

'Take a seat, Jenny,' Toni suggested as the phone rang again. 'Janet will see you shortly and Dr Cooper will check Melissa later.'

I hope, she added silently. Finishing the phone call, she watched as Janet bustled into the office.

'Is the recall list done?' the practice nurse queried.

'Right here.' Toni picked up the printout the computer supplied every Monday morning, detailing patients that needed recall for routine appointments such as smears, immunisations and blood tests. 'Have you seen Josh?'

'He's just parking his car.'

'Not like him to be late,' Toni said worriedly. 'I hope he's all right.'

'Nothing that fewer parties wouldn't cure, I'm sure,' Janet smiled. 'I'll bet he had a king-sized hangover yesterday after the wedding.'

'Wasn't it lovely?' Toni brightened. 'Oliver and Sophie looked so happy.'

'Mmm.' Janet was peering out of the office window. 'I don't think it rubbed off on the best man.' She turned away with a small sigh. 'Tell Jenny to come through to the treatment room any time.'

Josh stalked through the waiting area and into the office. He dropped the bag he was carrying and reached for one of the patient files in his basket, knocking over Toni's glass of water as he pulled it free.

'Oh, no!' Toni pounced to rescue the appointment book from the rapidly spreading puddle.

'Bloody stupid place to leave it,' Josh growled.

'Mrs Bradshaw is your first appointment,' Toni said calmly. 'Her file is on the top.'

Josh grunted. 'When's the locum turning up?'

'Not until this afternoon. A Dr Mareshka Singh.'

'Oh, great. I might just learn to pronounce his name by the time he leaves.'

'It's a she,' Toni corrected. Josh's patient was staring pointedly at them. 'Shall I take Mrs Bradshaw through to your room?'

Josh nodded. He used his foot to nudge the carrier bag he had dropped. 'Take care of this will you, Toni? It needs dry-cleaning.' The request was delivered with a smile which Toni couldn't help responding to. She looked more closely at Josh's face. His brown eyes were heavily shadowed and the lines the smile had brought out looked more pronounced than usual. Even the grey streaks in his curly brown hair seemed more obvious this morning.

'Would you like some coffee, Josh?'

'You're an angel, Swampy. Black. Two sugars.' Josh looked more cheerful as he headed off.

Toni dispatched Mrs Bradshaw, sent Jenny and her baby in to see Janet and greeted two more arrivals. The gardener came in at the same time.

'The hedge wants trimming,' he told her. 'Do you want me to do it now?'

'Yes, thanks, George.' Toni nodded. She switched the phone through to the staffroom and ducked away to make coffee for Josh.

When the jug refused to boil, Toni checked the light switches, to find that the power was off. A quick survey revealed the fault to be confined to the kitchen. Toni went back to the office and looked up the number for the electrician they used. Mrs Bradshaw was ready to pay her account. An indignant wail from the treatment room indicated that Josh was checking baby Melissa and her vaccinations were being attended to.

'I thought you were getting me some coffee?' Josh said plaintively as he came to collect the file on his next patient.

'The power's off,' Toni informed him. 'I'm working on it.'

'Have you checked the fuses?'

'No.' Toni gave him a level glance. 'I've called the electrician. He's on his way.'

Josh's mumble suggested that employing a tradesman was an unnecessary expense. Toni ignored him. She had far too much to do as it was, without trying to fiddle with the mysterious workings of a fuse box. It added an extra tension to an already difficult morning and Toni was feeling distinctly hassled by the time Josh emerged after his next patient.

'I've had Dr Braithewaite's receptionist on the phone. Bill Watson has an appointment with him this afternoon and they haven't received a referral letter. They want it faxed immediately.'

'Send it, then,' Josh said impatiently. 'What's the problem?'

'You haven't dictated it yet.'

'I did it on Friday.'

'No—I reminded you about it on Friday. Along with several others. You said—'

'The tape's on my desk,' Josh groaned. 'I must have forgotten to give it to you. Sorry.'

Toni simply nodded as she answered the phone again. Somehow she would have to find the time to type up the letter while trying to juggle more than the usual Monday morning rush. The absence of Oliver and Sophie had put pressure on them all. After several attempts, Toni finally fed the letter into the fax machine some time later, simultaneously coping with a phone call on the other line and directing a new arrival to take a seat. Having Josh glaring at the from the doorway did nothing to reduce the stress level.

'What's that infernal noise outside my window?'

'George is cutting the hedges.' Toni turned to the man leaning on the counter. 'Can I help you?'

'I've come about the power.' The electrician grinned cheerfully at Toni.

'Oh, that's great.' Toni returned the smile. 'The kitchen's at the end of the corridor.' Toni pointed towards the archway at the end of the counter. 'The fuse box is just outside Dr Spencer's consulting room.'

Janet's head appeared beside Josh. 'There's no hot water either, Toni.'

Josh shook his head disbelievingly. He chewed the inside of his cheek impatiently as Toni explained the location of the hot-water cylinder to the electrician, breaking in just as she finished.

'Get onto the after-hours clinic,' he ordered Toni. 'Mike Greaves had an ECG and bloods done over the weekend. I need the results.'

'OK, I'll see what I can do.' Toni was wondering which phone she should answer first.

'I need them *now*,' Josh snapped. 'I've got Mr Greaves sitting in my office. I need to know if there's been any change in his ECG since Saturday. He might need to be admitted to hospital.'

Toni sighed as one of the phones stopped ringing. Moving to answer the other phone, she stumbled against the bag Josh had left. Picking it up to get it out of the way, Toni looked inside. The bag contained a dark grey suit, probably the one Josh had worn at the wedding. The bag was close to her face, close enough to catch the scent of Josh still clinging to his clothes. Toni was still clutching the bag as she answered the phone. She jotted down the details of the call automatically. Maybe she could drop the suit at the dry-cleaners during her lunch-break. *If* she got a lunch-break.

The electrician came back. 'The element's blown in the hot-water cylinder,' he informed Toni. 'I'll have to drain the tank. You won't have any hot water till tomorrow.'

'What about the power?'

'That's back on. The element blowing just tripped an overload switch. You could have fixed that yourself.' The man's admiring smile suggested that Toni could tackle any task with ease. Toni suppressed a sigh.

'You can make coffee now,' the electrician said cheerfully. His smile broadened. 'Mine's white, no sugar.'

Toni stirred the mugs briskly a few minutes later. Was it any wonder she felt like a piece of furniture around here? Albeit a very capable piece of furniture. Toni could cope with anything. Even the electrician agreed. Would Josh even bother to thank her for his belated drink? Probably. His manners were usually impeccable but he would very likely use the opportunity to complain about the noise from the electric hedge-cutters, bemoan the absence of any hot water to wash his hands in and quite possibly also ask Toni to book a table at some exclusive restaurant for the date he had planned later in the week.

St David's couldn't have managed without her. Josh couldn't have managed without her. He'd told her often enough. For ten years, on and off, Toni had become more and more part of the fabric of the medical centre. It was her job. Her life. But just where was it headed? How long could she go on putting things right, making sure everything ran smoothly? Caring about someone who simply saw her as a necessary component of his working environment?

Maybe the changes Toni had made in her physical appearance had provoked a deeper change in her attitude to life. Or maybe the change in attitude had come first, sneaking up unobtrusively until the physical changes had made it obvious. What did it matter anyway? A fundamental change had occurred and Toni could feel a new tension gathering momentum.

She carried the mugs of coffee carefully. The electrician was enthusiastically cheerful. Josh's quiet smile and nod of thanks was far more effective. Toni closed the door of Josh's room slowly. Why was it that some things could change so dramatically while others seemed incapable of changing even a little?

Like the way Toni felt about Josh. Like the way he treated women in the same way he treated cars and fine wine and food. A necessary part of life but one that should never be mundane or predictable. The aspect of Josh that never changed was his need for constant change. New experiences. New cars...new women.

Josh's appreciation of new women was obvious when Toni rushed back from the dry-cleaners at the end of her lunch break to find their locum had arrived. Wearing a yellow sari beneath her white coat, Dr Mareshka Singh looked exotic and extraordinarily beautiful. The rope of braided, jet black hair hung to hip level and Toni instantly regretted cutting her own similarly dark, long tresses.

The bright yellow sari set off the dark, olive skin and the red dot on Dr Singh's forehead drew attention to her enormous black eyes. The Indian doctor's English was superb. Toni's fears that needing to assist the locum would add to her own and Janet's workload receded immediately.

'I've had at least a month's experience in general practice clinics in both Auckland and Wellington,' Dr Singh told them over a cup of coffee in the staff room. 'I'm trying all the main centres, before deciding where to settle. Then I'll send for my mother and the children.'

Josh was onto his second mug of coffee. Toni frowned as she saw he was still ignoring the sandwiches she had brought back from the local bakery. Josh nodded at his new locum.

'And your husband, Dr Singh?'

'Call me Mareshka, please. And I may call you Josh?'

'Of course.'

Toni's attention was caught by Janet's facial twitch. Their eyes met as Mareshka continued her conversation.

'My husband sadly died two years ago, Josh. I am looking for a new start for myself and my family.'

'I hope you find Christchurch to your liking, Mareshka. It's a lovely city.'

Janet excused herself and Toni followed suit. 'I'm sure Josh will look after you, Dr Singh,' Toni told the newcomer warmly, 'but, please, ask if there's anything I can do to help. We start the afternoon clinic at 1.30 p.m.'

Toni caught up with Janet just outside the door. They could both still hear Josh.

'We have a magnificent new Indian restaurant in the central city, Mareshka. Have you tried it yet?'

'No. I've only just arrived. I...' Mareshka Singh sounded hesitant.

'Perhaps I could have the pleasure of accompanying you.'

Josh's voice faded as Janet muttered to Toni, 'Doesn't waste much time, does he?'

'Life's too short to waste time,' Toni responded dryly. Josh's catch phrase jarred as she repeated it. Life *was* too short and she was only now becoming aware of how much of her own she was wasting. Had been wasting for ten years.

Was it really a whole decade since she'd responded to that advertisement in the local paper for a part-time receptionist at a medical centre? Toni plugged in her earphones, listening to Josh's voice on tape as she tapped busily on the computer keyboard, heading up the referral letter to a cardiology consultant.

'Re. Jacob Alan Donaldson,' she typed. 'Thank you for seeing this 72-year-old gentleman who is experiencing increasing shortness of breath on exertion.' Toni smiled at the quaint phrasing, though she was well used to the etiquette of medical professionals corresponding with each other. The assumption that their request to have their patient seen would be granted was polite but definite. Even if they disagreed over the treatment of a patient they usually managed to maintain an admirable civility.

Toni finished detailing the past medical history and current complaints of Mr Donaldson quickly. She glanced at the clock. With a bit of luck she might have time for another before anyone arrived for the afternoon surgery hours. It wouldn't take long. Toni's secretarial skills had been what had clinched this job for her in the first place. That, and the fact that she had been keen to move from her full-time job with a furniture removal company into part-time employment.

'My mother's not well,' she had told the young Dr

Cooper. 'I'd like to be able to spend more time caring for her.'

Josh had been sympathetic. He had wanted to offer assistance.

'Mum has been one of Dr Jamieson's patients for many years,' Toni had said. 'We don't live far away and she's not keen on changing medical centres.' She had hesitated but had known that her mother's file had been easily accessible to the doctor. 'My mother has Alzheimer's disease. I know I'm going to need help with her care eventually, but I'd like to manage by myself for as long as possible.'

Josh's understanding had made the position even more attractive to Toni. She had been proud to demonstrate her skill with computers. A skill which had increased markedly over the years, along with her knowledge and interest in the practice of medicine. With her current level of experience and expertise, Toni could probably get a job anywhere she wanted in the medical world.

The telephone rang before Toni could start her second letter. Then the first patient for the afternoon arrived and the lull in activity was over.

'How's the back, today, Mr Matthewson? Any better?'

The elderly man was lowering himself gingerly onto one of the waiting room chairs. 'Not so you'd notice.'

Toni tutted sympathetically. 'You'll have to take things a bit easier in your vegetable garden for a while. No heavy digging.'

'Had to get the compost in. It's time to plant the spuds. I'll bring you some nice little new kidney potatoes in September.'

'I'll look forward to it, Mr Matthewson.' Toni smiled but her expression changed to one of concern as she saw their patient wince. 'Dr Cooper won't be long.' She was reaching for the box of samples destined for the laboratory in town as she caught sight of a courier van pulling up on the roadside. There were more in the staffroom fridge.

'I'll just let Dr Cooper know you're here, Mr Matthewson,' Toni said helpfully. 'I'll be right back.'

The afternoon clinic ran like clockwork. Dr Singh saw almost as many patients as Josh and for once there were no emergencies to disrupt the appointment timetable. Janet left promptly at 5 p.m. to collect her sons as usual. Mareshka Singh left thirty minutes later.

'Would it be possible for me to have a key, please?' she asked Toni. 'I like to arrive early to be ready for the morning.'

'I'd need to show you the alarm system,' Toni said doubtfully. 'I'm always here by 8 a.m. The doctors don't normally arrive until 8.30 a.m.'

Josh had appeared from his office. 'That's right,' he assured the locum. 'We like to give Toni time to get the heaters going and boil the jug for the first round of coffees.'

Dr Singh inclined her head graciously. 'That's quite all right. I have no wish to disrupt your normal routine. I will arrive at 8.30 a.m.'

'We'll look forward to it.' Josh smiled. 'Thanks for your help today, Mareshka.'

'My pleasure, Josh. This is a pleasant clinic to work in.' Mareshka smiled at Toni. 'Your staff are excellent. I think Miss Marsh is capable of diagnosing and treating many of these patients herself. She knows them all so well.'

'Toni knows everybody well,' Josh agreed. 'And you're right. She's a treasure.'

Toni glanced at Josh suspiciously. Had the relatively calm afternoon improved his mood or was his good humour simply intended to charm the newcomer?

'Call me Toni, please, Dr Singh,' she directed. 'I only know people so well because I've been here for ever. Part of the furniture, really.'

Mareshka Singh raised an elegantly sculptured eyebrow. 'Furniture? I think not.' She smiled again, her sari rustling as she moved away.

Josh gave Toni a sharp glance after saying goodbye to his temporary colleague. 'What did you mean, part of the furniture, Swampy? You don't really believe that, do you?'

Toni shrugged. She gathered up the patient notes scattered on the counter and moved towards the shelf to file them. At least she'd intended to move towards the shelf. Josh was blocking her path. He stared down at her. An inch or two shorter than Oliver Spencer's six feet, Josh still towered over Toni's five feet, four inches. Toni surprised herself by the thought that she should really give up the flat shoes she wore for comfort at work. High heels were next on the list of changes. As though reading her thoughts, Josh frowned.

'I can't get used to you not wearing glasses,' he complained. 'And I can't help feeling I'm missing something else.' His frown deepened. 'You haven't gone and found yourself a man, have you?'

Toni gulped. Josh actually sounded almost...

jealous. Her voice—when it finally responded to her brain—sounded unnaturally high.

'Would it matter if I had?'

'Of course it would.' Josh was still staring down at her. Then he shook his head imperceptibly. 'Do you know, I've never really noticed the colour of your eyes before? They've got little flecks in them. Very unusual. Like a glass of whisky sitting in a shaft of sunlight.'

Toni laughed without amusement. The knowledge that Josh had seen her almost daily for ten years without noticing her eye colour was painfully revealing. Never mind the fact that her eyes had been disguised by prescription lenses until very recently. If he'd been interested he would have noticed.

'How romantic, Josh.' Toni didn't try and modify her sarcastic tone. 'Eyes like a glass of booze. A nickname that makes you think of alligators. No wonder you're so successful with women.' Toni made a decisive movement that caused Josh to step aside. He leaned back against the doorframe, watching as Toni stood on tiptoe and still had to stretch to slot her first patient file into place. His eyes narrowed slightly.

'So…it *is* a man, then?'

Toni poked the second file into place. 'Maybe I'm just having a mid-life crisis.'

'At thirty-five? I hope not. I'm sure you'll see more than three score and ten.'

'I'm thirty-three,' Toni snapped. God, he didn't even know how old she was.

'Oops, sorry.' Josh's grin was laced with a heavy dose of the charm he usually reserved for other women. Toni tried to ignore its impact and failed miserably.

'It's OK. What's a year or two between friends?' she mumbled. The third file went into place at the end of the shelf. Toni glanced at the file now in her hand. 'Don't you need to dictate a referral letter for Mrs Willis? I've made an appointment for her at the chest clinic.'

Josh reached out his hand to take the file. 'I'll do it right now.'

'No need.' Toni shook her head. 'The waiting list is terrible at this time of year. Her appointment's not for six weeks.'

'Oh, hell,' Josh muttered. 'She needs specialist assessment faster than that. Her emphysema is progressing too rapidly. What about going private?'

'She doesn't have insurance and she couldn't afford the fees. Her husband got laid off last year.'

'So? Book her in anyway,' Josh said imperiously. 'The practice can cover the cost.'

Toni raised an eyebrow but remained silent. She didn't need to remind Josh that he had a partner. Oliver had noted Josh's increasing habit of not charging patients who showed any evidence of financial hardship.

It wasn't that Oliver disagreed with the practice— he was simply concerned that some kind of policy was needed. Patients compared notes and Oliver had been put in the embarrassing position of having free consultations demanded by patients who were quite capable of paying the normal fee. It was usually Toni who caught the flak at the front desk and her silence must have reminded Josh that the subject had come up at a recent staff meeting.

'*I'll* cover the cost,' he said casually. 'It doesn't need to go anywhere near the practice books.'

Toni nodded. 'I'll see what I can do, then.' She shut down her computer and collected the ballpoint pens and pencils from her desk top, depositing them neatly into their holder. She closed the appointment book. 'That's us for today. I'm off home.'

'Mmm.' Josh hadn't moved. He was still leaning against the doorframe. 'This premature mid-life crisis of yours. It's not going to prompt any more major changes, is it?'

'Such as?' Toni fished under her desk for her shoulder bag.

'Like shifting house. Or changing jobs.'

'I'm not likely to shift. Imagine the criminal spree Bertie and Bessie would head into if I gave them fresh territory.'

Josh grinned. 'Haven't they grown out of that yet? You're the only person I've ever heard of who has cat burglars for pets.'

Toni shook her head. 'Burmese cats are a law unto themselves. Bertie came home with his sixteenth sock at the weekend.' She laughed. 'And we still haven't got a matching pair.'

'You can't shift house, then,' Josh said seriously. 'He'd never be able to find a matching set.' He stepped aside to let Toni out of the office. 'What about the job?'

'Furniture doesn't shift itself,' Toni pointed out. 'It gets shifted.' She glanced back over her shoulder. 'Sometimes it turns into an antique and becomes really valuable.'

It was Josh's turn to shake his head. 'OK, OK. So I got your age wrong. You don't need to rub my nose in it. I'm just rattled, that's all. Too many things are changing around here. Oliver getting married. You getting rid of your glasses. It's something in the air.'

'It's spring,' Toni informed him. 'Time to make some changes.'

Josh nodded almost with resignation and then sighed. 'Maybe I'll do some spring-cleaning in my office.'

'Yeah, right!' Toni walked briskly to the front door. She tossed a quick grin in Josh's direction. 'Even the cleaner's too scared to poke her duster too far into those piles. You've got ten years of spring cleaning to catch up on.'

Pulling open the door, Toni was startled by the sight of the man standing there with his hand raised. She took a step back.

'Sorry.' The man dropped his hand. 'I was going to knock. I know it's after hours.' He grinned at Toni. 'I was hoping you'd still be here, Toni.'

Toni gave Josh a questioning glance. He was staring suspiciously at the newcomer who was very tall and lean, with long blond hair drawn back into a ponytail. Josh clearly didn't recognise him either and he gave Toni a slight shake of his head.

'You don't remember me.' The man was still grinning. 'When Mum told me you were working here, I said that you wouldn't recognise me.'

'Your mum?' The voice *was* familiar. Toni bit her lip thoughtfully.

'The person who doesn't like mud pies even when they're decorated with crab apples.'

Toni gasped. *'Ben!'* She shook her head and laughed. 'I don't believe it! Why didn't your mum tell me you were coming home?'

'She didn't know. I only arrived a couple of days ago.'

'I've still got that postcard you sent me last year. Where was that from? Bolivia? China? I could never keep up with where you were.'

Ben shrugged and then smiled. 'I wouldn't have recognised you either, you know. Your hair's shorter.'

'And yours is longer,' Toni countered.

'You're not wearing your glasses any more.' Ben's look was appraising. 'You've turned into a real looker, Toni Marsh.'

This time it was embarrassment that prompted Toni to shake her head. It also reminded her that the conversation was being overheard. Turning to Josh, she discovered that his suspicious look had gone. Now he was radiating distinct disapproval.

'Josh, this is Ben Reynolds,' she informed him.

'How do you do?' Josh's nod was curt. 'I take it you know Toni.'

'Sure do. We held hands all the way home from our first date.'

Toni almost laughed again at Josh's expression. 'It was our first day at school.' Why did she feel the need to reassure Josh that Ben was simply an old friend? 'Ben lived down the same street. His mother is one of your patients, in fact. Janice Reynolds?'

The change in Josh's expression was instantaneous—from disapproval to neutrality and then to an alert interest that surprised Toni.

'I've heard about you.' Josh extended his hand. 'From what your mother's told me over the years, you've had some amazing adventures in your world travels.'

Toni watched the two men shake hands. She could

sense the rapport they felt. And why not? Ben had always had the same sort of attitude to life as Josh. He had just taken it closer to the edge—living hard, fast and dangerously in whatever exotic locations had taken his fancy.

'You've been away for ten years,' Toni observed curiously. 'Is this just a holiday?'

Ben shrugged. 'Who knows? Maybe I've got it all out of my system now and I'm ready to settle down.'

He didn't look too pleased at the prospect. Maybe some men were just born to go at life full tilt and could never be happy being caged in by too much stability. Men like Ben Reynolds. And Josh Cooper. Josh glanced at Ben and then at Toni.

'I'll leave you two to catch up, then,' he suggested. 'You must have a lot to talk about.'

Toni smiled. 'Like that mud pie we almost persuaded your mother to sample.'

Ben didn't respond. He had turned back to Josh. 'Actually, it was you I was hoping to talk to, Dr Cooper. Mum thinks it's high time I had a check-up after all the weird places I've been living in.'

Toni moved back towards the counter. 'Sounds like an excellent idea. I'll get the book out and make an appointment for you. When would you like it, Ben?' She looked back but this time neither of the men appeared to have heard her. Some communication had taken place between them which Toni had missed.

Josh spoke quietly. 'Why don't you come through now, Ben?'

'Are you sure? I don't want to keep you after hours, Dr Cooper.'

'I've got plenty of time.' Josh had his hand on Ben's shoulder as he guided him through the waiting room. 'And the name's Josh.' He glanced at Toni. 'You don't need to stay, Swampy. I'll lock up when we're through.'

'Swampy?' Ben sounded intrigued and then laughed. 'I wish I'd thought of that one.' His voice faded as he followed Josh down the hallway. '"Four-Eyes" was my unoriginal best.'

Toni sighed. The reminder of a detested childhood nickname shouldn't have to power to rankle now but it did. The nickname had never been used aggressively. She and Ben had been close friends until puberty had pushed them into differing social circles. Ben had been one of the most popular boys at high school, even when he'd got into trouble. It had been Ben Reynolds who'd been suspended for three days in the fifth form, having been caught smoking, and it had been Ben who'd been the star of the school's first fifteen rugby team. Faster, more daring and unwilling to even contemplate failure. He'd gone on to achieve everything he'd set out to do, pausing only long enough to set new and more exciting goals.

What had Toni achieved in the same period of time? A change of unattractive nickname and precious little otherwise. It wasn't just because it was spring. It was well past time for Toni to make some serious changes in her life, to set herself some new goals. Maybe this time she could come up with one that might be achievable.

CHAPTER THREE

WERE new resolutions contagious?

Toni was so used to watching Josh that she recognised subtle changes, even in mood, without trying. The changes that occurred for the remainder of that week were obvious enough even to rouse Janet Muir's curiosity.

'What *is* going on?' she asked Toni on Wednesday. 'All this stuff appearing from Josh's room.'

'He's spring-cleaning.' Toni pushed a large carton of medical journals more closely against the wall.

'Why?'

'Good question.' Toni sighed deeply. Josh's unusual preoccupation was adding to an already unsettled week. 'Don't worry, I think the novelty will wear off rapidly. He couldn't have picked a worse week to turn his office upside down. Dr Singh must think we're incredibly disorganised.'

'Ah!' Janet lowered her voice. 'Perhaps Josh is trying to impress our exotic visitor by making his consulting room habitable.'

'I don't think it's working, then.' Toni smiled wryly. 'She tripped over an empty oxygen cylinder he left outside his door yesterday and tore her sari. She wasn't very happy. I think she's trying to avoid him today.'

'Poor Josh,' Janet said with a grin. 'That'll be a bit of a shock to the system.'

Something was certainly disturbing Josh Cooper.

39

The gentle but firm rebuttal of any personal advance by Josh to Mareshka Singh wasn't enough to explain the clean-up. Or excuse the exacerbation of Josh's tendency to avoid or forget minor hassles. Toni's reminder lists were becoming longer. Some items were underlined and were still being ignored.

'I've got to have these cheques signed,' Toni told him firmly on Friday afternoon. 'And Janet's still waiting for you to check the drug supplies requisitions.'

'I'll get it done,' Josh said irritably. 'Don't nag me.'

'Someone has to,' Toni responded. 'I can't do it all myself.'

'You seem to manage.' Josh flashed a quick smile at her. 'I can't think of anyone else who nags me at all.'

'That's not what I meant.' How did he always manage to defuse any acrimony with that smile? 'The job's getting too big for me, Josh. I've told you we have to look at employing a receptionist. Do you know how often I have to stay late to get on top of the referral letters and the filing? I just don't get a chance during the day sometimes.'

'I know.' Josh looked contrite. 'We'll talk about it next week as soon as Oliver and Sophie get back. Don't worry, Swampy. We'll sort it out. Here, give me those cheques that need signing.'

Josh was still standing beside Toni, finishing the administrative chore, when the phone rang a few minutes later.

'I'm afraid Josh is fully booked for the rest of the day,' she said apologetically. 'Would Monday be all right?' Toni listened, a frown appearing on her face.

'Um…Ben?' she queried hesitantly. 'You haven't been drinking, have you?'

Josh virtually snatched the receiver from Toni's hand. 'I'll take that,' he snapped. 'Ben?' Josh sounded serious. He ignored Toni's stunned expression. 'Josh speaking. What's the problem?' He listened only briefly. 'Come in now,' he instructed. 'I'll see you straight away.'

'But you can't!' Toni protested as Josh put the phone down. 'We're overbooked as it is.' Her voice trailed off as she noted Josh's expression. 'What's so urgent, Josh? Is Ben ill?'

'You should know better than to ask a doctor to break rules about confidentiality,' Josh growled. 'I'm seeing him. That's all you need to know.' He flicked the pages of the appointment book. 'I'll see Mrs Grigg now before Ben gets here. Jason Weir just needs a repeat prescription.' He grabbed a pad and began scribbling. 'Get Janet to check his blood pressure and ask about any side effects. He'll just have to wait if he needs to be seen. I'm sure Mareshka can cope with anything else.' Josh turned away, stepping from the office door to the archway that framed the view of the well-patronised waiting room. 'Mrs Grigg? Come on through.'

Toni sighed heavily. She might as well forget about the farewell afternoon tea she had planned for Mareshka. The locum GP would have to spend her last hours at St David's working harder than she had all week. It was just typical of Josh. He decided what his priorities were and anyone around him simply had to fall in line and cope with any disruptions the decision caused. Why couldn't she be more like that?

Ben didn't look particularly ill but he did appear

withdrawn. He looked depressed, Toni decided, having quickly given up any attempts to chat with her childhood friend. Ben Reynolds clearly didn't feel like talking today and Toni was sharply reminded that she didn't really know him at all any more. Who knew what problems his lifestyle might have engendered? A drug habit—possibly. Or Aids. Or maybe alcoholism. His speech had definitely sounded a little slurred on the phone and he seemed to be slightly off balance when he responded to Josh's quiet invitation to go through to his consulting room a short time later.

A normal appointment was scheduled to last fifteen minutes. It wasn't unusual for a more serious case to run to thirty minutes. Rarely, the day's timetable could be thrown into chaos by a doctor spending forty-five minutes with one patient but Ben was still in Josh's office an hour and a half after he'd arrived. Janet had gone home. Even Mareshka had left, having dealt with the last of her extra patients with no complaint.

If Ben had looked withdrawn on his way in to see Josh, he looked totally exhausted on his way out. Neither man said anything to Toni but it wasn't their silence that she found disturbing. As familiar as she was with Josh's ability to empathise with his patients, there was something in his pale face that prompted Toni to follow him back to his office. She opened the door without knocking, unsurprised by the sight of Josh sitting with his face buried in his hands.

'What's going on, Josh? What's wrong with Ben?'

Josh lifted his head and sighed wearily. 'I can't tell you that, Toni. You know that.'

'Oh, for God's sake, Josh. I'll be able to read his

notes as soon as you've written them. I'll have to type up any referral letters you intend to send. I've known Ben practically all my life. Janice Reynolds has been like a mother to me ever since my own mother got ill more than ten years ago. I *care* about these people.'

Josh regarded her steadily. 'How well did you know Ben's father, Toni?'

Surprised by the question, Toni sat down slowly on the chair Ben must have been using. It was still warm.

'He died about the time Mum got sick. Just before Ben left to go overseas.'

'I know.' Josh nodded. 'But how well did you know him before that? How much did you know about what killed him?'

Toni swallowed painfully. 'It was horrible. He had Huntington's disease.'

'I know that, too,' Josh said impatiently. 'How much do you know about the disease?'

'Quite a lot, actually.' Toni was nettled by Josh's tone. Was he implying that she wouldn't understand whatever problems Ben was having because she had no medical training? 'Huntington's chorea is a hereditary disease,' she said coolly. 'If one of your parents has it, you have a fifty per cent chance of inheriting it. Onset usually occurs between the ages of thirty and fifty. The average age of onset is thirty-eight.' Toni brushed a stray curl back from her face. 'Jim Reynolds was thirty-nine when his symptoms became apparent. Ben was only seven. I was there when it happened.'

Josh frowned sharply. 'What do you mean, you were *there*? It's hardly an instantaneous process. Quite the opposite. It takes about—'

'About ten years,' Toni interrupted angrily. 'I *know*

that, Josh. Over a ten-year period, a person with Huntington's loses the ability to walk, to speak, to swallow—even to think. It's a death sentence that tortures before it kills and there's no effective treatment or cure. The victim is locked inside a body that freezes up and tries to choke or suffocate them. Nobody really knows how aware they are.'

Josh's gaze was locked on Toni's with a peculiar intensity. 'OK,' he said quietly. 'You know a bit more than I thought you would. So what did you mean by saying you were there when it happened?'

'Ben and I were building a hut in his back garden. It was a Saturday afternoon. We needed a hammer and nails so we went into the shed to ask his dad. Jim Reynolds was doing something with his electric drill and he was trying to pick up a bit. His fingers were shaking so much he couldn't get it out of the box and he got terribly angry. He hurled the box of attachments across the room and then threw the entire drill after them.'

Toni glanced up at Josh to see whether she was taking too long with her story to interest him. His gaze was still locked on her face. He raised his eyebrows, encouraging her to continue.

'Ben and I were terrified. We'd never seen him angry like that, but what was even worse was that when he saw us watching him he began to cry. I'd never seen a man cry before.' Toni looked away from Josh. 'I've never forgotten that afternoon.'

'Neither has Ben,' Josh offered quietly.

Toni nodded. 'I'm not surprised if it's still affecting him. He was devastated by it all. When the diagnosis was made and they were told it was incurable, Ben wouldn't believe it. He told me that he was going to be a doctor when he grew up. *He* was going to find the cure for Huntington's.'

Josh smiled almost wistfully but his gaze still hadn't left Toni's face. 'It must have been a terrible time for Ben and his mother.'

'It was ghastly,' Toni agreed softly. 'He began having trouble swallowing, which would make him choke. My mother and I were there for dinner one night and he ended up vomiting on the table. I don't think they ever had guests for dinner again. He started staggering when he walked. He looked as though he were drunk. Ben was out with him one night and the police picked him up. They wouldn't believe Ben when he said that his father was sick, and they locked him up until Janice was able to get to the police station. That was when Ben was about fourteen. He got really angry with his father after that and wouldn't let me visit his house any more.'

'Why not?'

'I think he was embarrassed. His dad couldn't work. He couldn't help around the house. He couldn't even remember which drawer his socks were in or the way to the bathroom. He couldn't carry on a conversation without forgetting what he was talking about. Janice refused to let him be put into a nursing home until she simply couldn't cope any more, and that wasn't until Ben had left home to go to university.'

'Did Ben talk about it much?'

Toni shook her head. 'Not to me. There was a long time, after his father was arrested, when Ben didn't want to talk to me at all. I knew too much, I suppose, and he didn't want anyone at school talking. It was Janice who told me how hard he'd found it to make a decision about getting himself tested. I couldn't understand that. Imagine having to live with the possibility that such a horrible fate was waiting for you.'

'Imagine,' Josh echoed grimly.

'Janice was terrified as well.' Toni cleared her throat. 'Thank God the result was negative. Ben wasn't carrying the gene.' She smiled a little wearily at Josh but his face remained still.

'Ben never had himself tested, Toni.'

'Yes, he did. He told me the results himself. And Janice was so relieved. She didn't know how she could have lived with the uncertainty if he hadn't had the test.'

'Perhaps that's why he lied.'

'But he didn't,' Toni insisted. 'He couldn't have.' She bit her lip as the implication of what Josh was suggesting sank in. 'Why would he have done that?' she whispered eventually.

'Ben told me he couldn't have lived with the knowledge that his father's fate was also going to be his,' Josh told her gently. 'He said he decided that he'd rather live in hope that he might be all right, otherwise he wouldn't really be living at all.'

'But he went through all the counselling sessions. Janice went with him to some of them.'

'He withdrew from the testing process before the final blood test. He was only twenty, Toni. He decided that he had maybe twenty years to make the most of life and at least have some hope that he wasn't affected. If, or when, symptoms became apparent, he planned to kill himself.'

Toni gasped. 'He wouldn't do that!'

Josh shrugged. 'Why not? Is killing yourself more horrific than allowing a disease to do it a lot more slowly and painfully?'

Toni stared at Josh silently for a long moment. 'I guess not,' she admitted reluctantly. 'Not if you know for certain.'

'Ben thinks he does know.'

'Oh, God!' Toni closed her eyes briefly. 'Is that why he came home?'

'Probably. He's very scared.'

'Is he going to get himself tested now?'

'We're discussing it. It's possible his symptoms may be due to other causes.'

'What symptoms? His speech? Is that why I thought he'd been drinking when he rang?'

Josh nodded. 'He's having difficulty swallowing on occasion. And he loses his balance sometimes.'

'What other causes could there be?'

'Parkinson's maybe. Or alcoholism. Possibly even a viral illness.'

'But you don't think that's likely.' Toni searched Josh's face somberly.

'Unfortunately, no.'

Toni pressed her fingertips to her forehead as she bent her head. 'Poor Ben,' she said sadly. 'And poor Janice.' Toni was unprepared for the tears she felt gather and roll down her cheeks. She was also unprepared for the soft touch of Josh's hands as he pulled her up and into his arms.

'I'm sorry, Toni. I know, it's hard on everyone who cares.'

Josh cradled her head on his shoulder and Toni gave herself up to the luxury of being held and comforted. There was nowhere else she could want to be right then. Nowhere else she could ever want to be. Were some of her tears acknowledging the fact that she didn't really have the right to be there? Toni pulled back a little.

'I'm sorry. I really didn't think it would hit me this hard.' Toni took a shaky breath. 'It's not as though we've been really close in recent years. It's just that I thought it was all over years ago for Ben and Janice. That fear…'

'I know.' Josh smoothed Toni's hair away from her face.

'Maybe he won't get it as badly as his father did. Maybe it's not the start of Huntington's at all. He's still much younger than the average age of onset.' Toni looked at Josh questioningly. 'Does Janice know?'

'Not yet.' Josh stepped back. 'That's another consultation I'm not looking forward to. Ben doesn't want her to know yet.' He glanced at Toni, frowning. 'He didn't want anybody to know. He only came to me because he was desperate.'

Toni smiled gently. 'He certainly picked the right doctor to come to.'

Josh gave her an odd look. 'Why do you say that?' he queried sharply.

'Because you care,' Toni replied simply. 'And I think you understand what he's going through. What Janice will have to go through.'

'Oh, yes.' Josh turned away from her and Toni could sense his withdrawal in more than a physical sense. 'I understand only too well.' He shut the case notes on his desk with an angry movement. 'Unfortunately, I doubt that my understanding is likely to make much of a difference. To anyone.'

'Yes, it will,' Toni stated firmly. 'It already has,'

she added more quietly as she turned to leave. 'To me.'

Spring-cleaning definitely had a therapeutic side. Toni spent the weekend attacking shelves and cupboards in her house that hadn't had any attention for years. She excused her enthusiasm by admitting her distress over what was lying in store for the Reynolds family. On a deeper level she recognised that she was channelling her own frustration over her job and her relationship with Josh into her ceaseless activity. Whatever was really prompting the clean-out didn't matter. It was working. Toni even decided to add the carton of feline contraband from the laundry to the final carload destined for the rubbish tip. Bertie and Bessie appeared unmoved by Toni's lecture as she stirred the contents of the box.

'This has got to stop,' she warned the cats. 'Do you have any idea how embarrassing it would be if the neighbours found out?' She dropped the worn gym shoe and pulled another item from beneath the pile of socks. 'What on earth possessed you to drag a pair of trackpants home, Bertie? Or was that one a joint effort?'

The cats groomed seal brown fur with practised precision and ignored their owner. She might seem displeased but they knew exactly how welcome they'd be when they curled up in her lap to keep her company later that evening. Toni disappointed her pets, however, by failing to settle until she was too exhausted to do anything but fall into bed.

By Monday morning the house was cleaner than it had been in decades and Toni felt much more at peace with herself and her world. She was ready to make a start to a new phase in her life, ready to welcome Oliver and Sophie Spencer back to St David's and cope with the support she knew Janice Reynolds might well need in the near future.

Patients who had put off their appointments rather than see a locum made Monday an exceptionally busy day. Janice Reynolds rang early to make an appointment to see Josh, but the dampening of the atmosphere Toni experienced was counterbalanced by the pleasure of having the full team together again and hearing details of the honeymoon which both Oliver and Sophie related with glowing appreciation.

'Rudyard Kipling described Milford Sound as the eighth wonder of the world,' Sophie told Toni and Janet later in the morning. 'It's unbelievably beautiful. Mountains, forests, lakes. We took a cruise out to Doubtful Sound and another one on Milford Sound. I lost count of the number of waterfalls we saw. We even had a whole pod of dolphins chasing the boat.' Sophie smiled happily at the memory. 'Oliver nearly fell overboard, trying to take photographs.'

'A cruise sounds good.' Janet nodded. 'Must have been a bit cold, though. Did you get much rain?'

'Heaps,' Sophie admitted. 'But that's part of the beauty of Fiordland. When it rains you get more and more waterfalls. And it wasn't bad enough to stop us tramping. We walked up to Lake Marian and tried the start of the Hollyford Track.'

'Did you walk the Milford Track?' Janet queried. 'I've often thought I'd like to take the boys on that one when they're old enough.'

'It's not open at this time of year.' Sophie peered at the patient file in her in-basket but made no move to collect it. 'We've booked in to do it over summer.'

She grinned. 'We figured we'd be ready for a second honeymoon in about six months.'

'Tramping isn't exactly my idea of a romantic honeymoon,' Toni mused. 'I'd prefer something tropical. Lazing about on a beach, under some palm trees.'

'Try lazing about after walking hard all day in the rain and then having a hot bath outside under the stars.' Sophie caught sight of Oliver as he entered the office and her cheeks went a little pinker. 'It takes some beating,' she murmured.

'What would take some beating?' Oliver enquired.

'The number of appointments to get through today.' Toni handed each doctor a patient file. 'Honeymoon's over, I'm afraid.'

'No.' Oliver shook his head as he stood back to let Sophie go ahead of him. 'We're on permanent honeymoon. It's just the holiday that's over.'

By the end of the day both Spencers had decided that the holiday was definitely over and that they needed another one.

'Sorry.' Toni smiled. 'Not a chance. Did Josh remind you about the staff meeting at 8 a.m. tomorrow?'

Oliver and Sophie both nodded then exchanged meaningful glances. Oliver turned back to Toni. 'Is there anything wrong with Josh?'

'What do you mean?' Toni's eyes widened at the concern she saw in Oliver's face.

'He looks awful,' Oliver said quietly. 'After a week away I got quite a shock, seeing him this morning. I'm sure he's lost weight and he's very pale.'

Sophie nodded vigorously. 'I thought so, too. And he seems terribly quiet.'

Toni stared at them. Josh *had* seemed subdued

around her but she'd assumed it had been due to the impact the Reynolds case was having. She wouldn't have expected Josh's concern for his patients to have stifled his welcome for the return of his colleagues. 'Did you talk to him about it?'

Oliver laughed ruefully. 'You know Josh.'

'Mmm.' Toni smiled, trying to quell the twinge of alarm she experienced. 'He takes any enquiry about his health with the same grace as a personal insult.'

'His office looks like a bomb's gone off in there.' Oliver shook his head with disbelief. 'There are odd boxes lying all over the place and I found an empty oxygen cylinder in the hot-water cupboard of all places.'

Toni smiled. 'Josh got sick of spring-cleaning. He was quite enthusiastic for a day or so.'

Oliver's eyes widened. 'The fact that he was interested at all is pretty weird.'

'Maybe he's having problems with his love life,' Sophie suggested. 'From what Janet told me, it sounds as if your locum was rather gorgeous.' She nudged Oliver. 'Maybe he's not very pleased to see us back so soon.'

'Huh!' Toni's tone was dismissive. 'If a woman was responsible for disturbing Josh Cooper's peace of mind, I'd eat my hat. It's more likely that his lifestyle is finally catching up with him. Who knows what he got up to over the weekend?'

The sound of Josh's door closing precipitated an exchange of guilty glances. Josh gave his colleagues a surprised stare as he reached the office door.

'My ears are burning,' he murmured. 'I hope you were all saying nice things about me.'

There was a moment's awkward silence.

'We're worried about you.' Sophie ignored Oliver's warning frown. 'You're looking a bit peaky.' Her expression informed Josh that she was quite ready to stand up to any aggravation her comment might provoke, but Josh grinned broadly.

'Peaky? I'll bet you got top marks in your course on advanced medical terminology.' He shook his head, still smiling. 'You'll be prescribing me a tonic next.'

Sophie glared at him. 'Cod liver oil,' she muttered. 'Five times a day.'

'Syrup of figs is good,' Toni offered, relieved that Josh had accepted the concern with good humour. 'I even found a bottle of it when I was spring-cleaning yesterday. Mum must have had it tucked away for at least twenty-five years.'

'Wow!' Oliver slapped Josh on the back. 'Vintage figs. Sounds right up your street, mate.' His concern for his colleague's state of health had clearly diminished. 'Get a good night's sleep,' he advised. 'It's certainly what I need after today. Come on, Sophie. It's time to go home.'

'A good night's sleep?' Sophie followed Oliver through the archway into the waiting room. 'You make it sound like we've been married for twenty years.'

Josh and Toni couldn't hear the response that Oliver bent down to whisper in Sophie's ear but the newly wed couple were both laughing as they went out, arm in arm.

Toni found the atmosphere changed the instant the door shut. Josh Cooper was also on the point of leaving.

'How's Janice?' Toni queried cautiously.

'Fine. She gave her wrist a bit of a sprain, gardening, over the weekend. She's a bit worried about Ben but thinks he might be withdrawn because he's bored by being back at home. It's only a matter of time before she learns the truth, I expect.'

'I must go and see her,' Toni decided aloud. 'It's ages since we had a good chat and I could do with some new cuttings for my garden.'

'Just watch what you say,' Josh warned.

'Don't worry, I'm not going to speak out of turn.' Toni looked away and sighed. 'I just wish there was some way of helping. Janice has been so good to me. I care about her a lot. And I'm worried about her.'

'You worry about a lot of people.' Josh smiled. 'It's one of the things that makes you special. Are *you* OK?'

Toni nodded. The depth of caring she saw in Josh's face brought a lump to her throat. She wished, with quiet desperation, that the base prompting the concern could have been more than friendship. But she knew it couldn't. Toni swallowed the lump carefully.

'I'm fine, thanks, Josh.' She held the eye contact. 'Are *you* OK?'

Their gazes held for a long moment, long enough for Toni to feel that the communication was deeper than any spoken words could have been, that the connection was drawing them close enough for their souls to touch. The power of the attraction was far greater than anything physical could have been but the pain as Josh broke the contact was astonishingly physical.

'I'm fine, too,' Josh said lightly. 'Don't worry about me, Toni.'

Her concern had been dismissed. The connection

rejected. Toni sat quietly for some minutes after Josh left. Had she imagined the step they'd taken towards each other? The recognition of something far, far deeper than friendship? No. It had been real. Real enough for Josh to recognise it as well. Real enough to make him run for cover. It was the clearest indication Toni had ever had that her feelings might not be welcome. Yet Josh had felt something, too. Was he simply afraid to acknowledge a new discovery or was he strengthening his resolve to let nothing come of it? Toni was left with an escalating tension. Something which had been left to simmer for far too long was about to boil dry. Or ignite.

The status quo had just become untenable.

CHAPTER FOUR

'WHAT *is* Josh doing out there?' Oliver Spencer peered through the staffroom window into the car-parking area at 7.55 the following morning. 'He's just standing there, staring at his car.'

'Probably thinking about trading it in,' Toni quipped. 'After all, he's had it for at least two months. There must be a sexier model available by now. Is one of those for me, by any chance?'

'Of course.' Oliver stopped pouring the percolated coffee and handed Toni a mug. 'And here's yours, Sophie.' Oliver's face lit up as his wife entered the room. He bent his head to drop a light kiss on her lips as soon as she came close enough.

Toni looked away, feeling distinctly excluded. She took her coffee to the table and sat down.

'Where's Janet?' Sophie sat down beside her.

'She'll be late. In fact, she's asked if we could schedule the staff meetings for another time. She can't make it in by 8 a.m., what with having to get the boys to school. It's one of the topics I want to bring up.'

'Eight-thirty never gave us long enough,' Oliver reminded her. 'We always ended up running late or not finishing.' He put a mug of black coffee at the end of the table where Josh usually sat, then settled himself opposite Sophie.

Josh was shaking his head as he came in. 'You'll never believe what I just did.' He picked up the black coffee and took an appreciative swallow. 'Ah, wonderful. Who needs breakfast?'

'You do by the look of it. You're fading away,' Oliver told his senior partner. He was rewarded with a contemptuous snort.

'So what have you just done?' Sophie queried.

Josh looked embarrassed. 'Locked my keys in the car.'

Oliver laughed. 'How on earth did you manage that? I would have thought there'd be an idiot-proof system built in.'

'I can't remember.' Josh sounded faintly puzzled now. 'But there it is. I'm locked out.'

'Forgetfulness is the first sign, you know.' Sophie said knowingly.

'The first sign of what, precisely?' Something in Josh's tone made everyone feel uncomfortable. It reminded them of the potential ill humour Sophie had risked the previous evening, having had the temerity to question Josh's physical well being.

'Uh...of not having breakfast?' Sophie looked at Oliver but he was exchanging meaningful glances with Toni. Josh missed none of the byplay.

'Let's get on with this, shall we?' Josh suggested coolly. 'Toni, as soon as we're through, call the Automobile Association for me and get them to come and unlock my car. My membership card's in my wallet.'

Toni made a note on her pad. 'I'll try and find the time,' she agreed. Josh stared at her.

'Please do,' he said crisply. 'I'll probably have some house calls later and I don't fancy waiting around for taxis. Now, what's the first item on the agenda?'

'A new receptionist,' Toni said promptly. She had written the agenda herself.

'You're not leaving, are you, Toni?' Oliver sounded horrified.

'No. Although that might be one solution.' Toni couldn't believe she'd said the words aloud. It wasn't something she'd ever really contemplated. The play of expressions on Josh's face in reaction to her casual words was startling. He looked as horrified as Oliver but then a shadow fell that made him look as though the idea was almost a relief. The reaction was gone in an instant, replaced by a guarded neutrality.

'What are you trying to say, Toni?'

'That I'm swamped.' Toni didn't recognise the play on her nickname until everybody laughed. The tension eased suddenly.

'Do you realise we've now got well over two thousand family files on our books and that the number of casuals is increasing steadily?' Toni allowed her gaze to travel around the group. 'I need at least part-time help with reception or I can't do my job as practice manager properly.'

'Fine. You should go ahead and advertise, then,' Josh decided. 'What do you think, Oliver?'

'Of course.' Oliver nodded. 'We can't have Toni stressed out. Imagine the chaos we'd all be in if she did decide to leave?'

'Hmm.' Josh sounded impatient. 'What's next on the list, Toni?'

Janet Muir arrived at 8.40 a.m., just as the main business of the meeting had been concluded.

'Sorry,' she apologised. 'What have I missed?'

'We saved the most important bit,' Oliver assured

her. He drew a large envelope from his briefcase. 'Wedding photos!'

They were soon spread over the table with many exclamations, reminiscences and admiring comments from Toni and Janet. Josh was unusually silent. He picked up one of the photographs and studied it intently, then discarded it back onto the pile. Toni's gaze followed the movement and she drew the photo closer.

The picture was one of herself and Josh. He was looking down at her, a gentle smile on his face. She was gazing up, her lips parted, and she had an almost beseeching expression. Toni remembered exactly when the photograph must have been taken. Josh had just confessed the horror of imagining the wedding to be his own. Toni had been wondering whether his attitude hadn't been at least partly put on. The photograph had captured another interpretation entirely. It looked as though Toni was gazing lovingly up at a man who felt exactly the same way she did.

'Isn't that lovely?' Sophie tapped the photo Toni was holding. 'You'll have to put it up on your noticeboard. You look like the perfect couple.'

Toni noticed how quickly Josh excused himself. 'I think I'll settle for one of you and Oliver,' Toni told Sophie quietly. 'The genuine perfect couple.'

The AA man arrived and unlocked the door of Josh's car at 10 a.m.

'Better keep a spare around,' he advised Josh. 'In case it happens again.'

'I'll get one cut,' Josh agreed. 'And give it to Toni here. She looks after me.' The smile Toni received was sincerely appreciative. At one time the glow the smile provoked could have kept Toni happy for days. This time it wore off in seconds.

'Josh? Have you got a minute?'

'For you, Swampy? Any time.' Josh leaned against the doorframe of Toni's office.

'I've got Cashmere Pharmacy on the phone. They're querying the script you gave Mrs Bell this morning. Did you really want her to take 100 mg, four times a day?'

'What?' Josh's brow creased. 'Don't be ridiculous. It's a divided dose. 25 mg, four times a day—100 mg in total.'

'That's not what you put on the script.'

'Nonsense. I remember writing the damned thing. Perhaps the pharmacist needs glasses.'

'They faxed a copy through before they rang.' Toni held out the piece of paper.

Josh stared at it, still frowning. Toni felt disquieted. It had been an easy enough error to have made but the implications been serious and it was lucky the pharmacist had spotted it. The mistake was also entirely out of character for Josh and it couldn't be blamed on indecipherable handwriting. He had an unusually tidy style for a doctor. Toni watched and waited, startled when Josh decisively shredded the paper with quick movements and let them shower into the waste-paper basket. 'I'll write another one,' he growled. 'You can fax it through in a minute.'

Toni was still watching Josh as he left. She uncovered the mouthpiece of the phone she held. 'Sorry to keep you waiting,' she said pleasantly. 'You were quite correct. The dosage should be 25 mg, four times a day. Dr Cooper is redoing the prescription now.'

She faxed through the revised dosage a few

minutes later. Josh had said nothing, merely slapping the paper down on the counter, exchanging it for a new patient file.

'Denise?' he called over the counter into the waiting room. 'Come on through. Sorry to have kept you waiting.'

Josh still didn't have anything to say to Toni as his patient left and he collected the request for a house call. Oliver was in the office at the same time.

'It's Bob Granger,' Josh muttered, showing the note to Oliver. 'He went into the hospice for a few days to give Diane a break and they've adjusted his morphine pump again. He went home last night and it sounds like he's in a bad way.'

'Oh, no.' Oliver sighed. 'Diane was determined not to put him in the hospice at all. I saw her a couple of weeks ago and she was exhausted. It was me who persuaded her to try the hospice at least for a day or two. Bob's already hung on for months longer than anyone expected, and who knows how much longer it will go on? I don't suppose she'll consider a break again after this.'

'I'll talk to her,' Josh promised. 'Don't blame yourself, Oliver. I would have suggested the same thing myself.'

Both doctors looked preoccupied and dispirited and Toni wished there was something she could do to help Josh. No wonder he'd been forgetful over his car keys and had made that error on Mrs Bell's prescription. He couldn't help but get emotionally involved with seriously ill patients. Like Bob Granger. And Ben Reynolds. He gave his support unstintingly at times like this and did it better than anyone else she could think of.

Toni watched him leave the office, remembering how Josh had supported her through many difficult times. He'd allowed her to fit her hours around the times her mother had gone to the day care facility in the early years. He'd never complained when she hadn't been able to make it into work because of some crisis with her mother's health or emotional state. There had just been the two of them at St David's then. A team that had worked together with remarkable tolerance.

It had been Josh who'd diagnosed her mother's stroke. The unexpected complication had left her entirely dependent on Toni physically and had accelerated the intellectual effects of the Alzheimer's. Josh had been upset but still supportive when Toni had made the difficult decision to leave work and care for her mother full time.

She'd seen him quite frequently over the next year as he'd provided the medical care her mother had needed, medical care which had become increasingly difficult to provide at home. Toni hadn't expected that caring for her mother would have been so demanding. Or needed for such a long time. She'd become frustrated and unhappy.

It had been Josh who'd finally persuaded her to put her mother into the rest home which had excellent hospital facilities. He'd also wanted her to come back to work full time at St David's. Josh had been about to take on Oliver Spencer as a partner. The practice had been taking off and he'd wanted more than a receptionist.

'I need someone I can trust,' he told her. 'Someone I know I can work with. You'll be the practice manager, Toni. I need you.'

How could she turn down the appeal? To be needed by Josh was more than Toni had ever expected. She went back to St David's eagerly, assuaging her guilt over abandoning her mother by spending her evenings at the rest home. Then her mother died and it was Josh that Toni turned to for comfort. She was embarrassed by how devastated she felt.

'It's not as though she's even known who I was since the stroke,' she reminded Josh. 'And this was hardly unexpected.'

Josh held her close. 'It's always hard to lose a parent, no matter how expected—or even welcomed—it is. It's even harder when you can't get close enough to say goodbye.'

Toni nodded. Trust Josh to understand

'It gives you even more to deal with, doesn't it?' he suggested gently. 'The anger that they've retreated from you. The guilt of not being able to feel the same love or being able to care for them.'

Toni was moved by his empathy. 'You sound like you've been there, Josh.' She'd never been given any more than snippets of a personal history from Josh. Toni wanted to know more, to extend the closeness the opportunity presented. But Josh backed off with a comment to the effect that he'd seen it all too often through his patients.

Now he was offering the same kind of empathy to Diane Granger. Perhaps it was just his professional personality. Did patients fall in love with Josh, believing that the depth of concern might touch a personal level? Or was it just that Toni's exposure over such a length of time had made it inevitable in her case?

She had never been able to return the support on a

personal level. Her only expression of caring had been confined to the professional arena, and she'd been happy to do whatever she'd been able to make life a little easier for him. Perhaps if she hadn't been so helpful Josh would have been forced to have seen her as something more than a useful colleague. Had her tolerance created Josh's expectations that she would always smooth over his casual attitude to the more mundane aspects of human existence? That she would always care about him whether or not he returned the sentiment?

It wasn't just today's small irritations that bothered Toni. It was her own ability to excuse Josh and go right on caring, her ability to make and then shelve the resolution to get herself out of her emotional rut. Toni ploughed through an afternoon's work, unsuccessfully trying to shake her annoyance with herself. When Oliver left for the day, giving Toni his afternoon case notes for filing, Toni redirected her annoyance towards Josh. No doubt his patient files would be scattered all over his room. If she didn't collect them herself she would be hunting for them in a hurry some time over the next day or two.

Catching her ankle on the box of out-of-date journals, still sitting where Josh had abandoned them was the last straw. He was probably waiting for Toni to finish his spring-cleaning. What was worse, she would probably take pleasure in being able to help. It was really quite pathetic. Having marched down the hallway, Toni rapped sharply on Josh's door. He was in front of his computer. The screen showed a small, brightly coloured creature being chased by equally lurid monsters.

'Oh, no! I'm dead—again!' Josh exclaimed. He

looked up at Toni with a boyish grin. 'This is a hard game. Do you think the twins will like it?'

Toni ignored the query. Janet's children were rapt with any attention they got from Josh when they visited the clinic. Toni had always enjoyed seeing Josh interact with the small and lively boys. She knew he loved children even if he no desire to become a father himself. Right now she was too fed up with her relationship with this man to allow herself to be sidetracked into the more positive aspects of his personality.

'You've seen twenty-eight patients today,' she told Josh coldly. 'I'm missing twenty-eight files. Is it too much to ask for you to at least put them in my office?'

Josh blinked in surprise. 'I guess I forgot.'

'You always forget,' Toni snapped. 'Just like you forget to take your coffee-mugs back to the kitchen.' She waved her hand at the collection dotting the surface of Josh's desk. 'And like you forget your hairdressing appointments and lunch dates if I don't happen to remind you. I'll bet you've forgotten you even intended to spring-clean your office and now you're quite happy to leave it half-done. You'd forget to eat lunch if I didn't buy it for you. It's no wonder you're looking sick.'

'I am *not* looking sick,' Josh said indignantly.

'Oh, yes, you are. Even Oliver's worried about you. You've lost weight, you look terrible and you're doing strange things.'

'Like what?' Josh said angrily. 'What the hell's got into you, Toni? What have I done that's so *strange*?'

'You locked yourself out of your car.'

'Big deal,' Josh scoffed.

'You stuffed up the dosage on that prescription.'

Toni's anger turned suddenly to concern. 'That's not like you, Josh. What's the matter?'

The muscles of Josh's face bunched. He looked furious. 'What is this? Some kind of personal inquisition? It's hardly worth a complaint to the medical council. Are you saying I'm not doing my job properly?'

'No, I'm not. I'm concerned about you, Josh.' Toni raised her voice, trying to get her message across. 'We all are.'

'Well, you can all mind your own bloody business.' Josh snatched the patient files off his desk. 'Look, I'll file the damned things myself. You can go home.' He pushed his chair back and jerked to his feet. 'For God's sake, Toni. You sound like a nagging wife. You forgot your coffee-cup, you forgot to put your files away.' His voice rose in an unpleasant mimicry of Toni's. 'Next you'll be telling me I drink too much.'

'Perhaps you do.' Toni was stung by the criticism. 'Perhaps that's what the problem is.'

'I don't *have* a bloody problem,' Josh shouted.

Toni flinched and her face paled. Josh had never shouted at her before. Never. As though appalled at himself, Josh rubbed at his forehead with his palm.

'Look, I'm sorry,' he mumbled. 'But I'm not in the mood for this and I can't understand where you're coming from. You think *I'm* doing strange things.' His glance at Toni was pained. 'It's hardly like you to lay into me. I thought we understood each other better than that.'

'I thought so, too.' Toni was still shocked at the way Josh had spoken to her. 'Perhaps we don't after all.'

'I'm sorry,' Josh repeated. 'It hasn't been a great day. It was a difficult visit with Diane Granger and I've got Ben Reynolds's case on my mind.'

'Forget it,' Toni said hurriedly. She had to look away from the appeal in Josh's eyes. 'It doesn't matter.'

'It does matter.' Josh was frowning heavily as he walked towards Toni. He drew her into a gentle hug. 'It matters a lot. I had no excuse to take things out on you. I care about you far too much to do that.'

Toni twisted in his arms and raised her face. Had she heard that correctly? Did he *really* care that much? Her eyes met his, appealing for confirmation, her lips parted as she tilted her head back to make eye contact. She could see distress darkening his eyes to a new depth of brown. She could see his concern. And she could see...

She could see nothing. The distance between their faces closed and she felt the tentative brush of Josh's lips on her own. A fleeting touch. Too brief. Toni could feel his mouth hovering over hers, ready to descend again. When it did, she knew she would be lost. It would be a real kiss. Maybe one that neither of them could control. But the space remained.

'I'm sorry,' Josh repeated.

Toni opened her eyes. 'It's all right, Josh. I shouldn't have gone on at you. I'm sorry, too. It's just...'

'Just what?' Josh prompted warily.

'Just that I care about you.' Toni's heart thumped painfully. 'A lot,' she added almost inaudibly.

She could sense his withdrawal even before he let go of her.

'I'm fine,' he said dismissively. 'I'm just sorry I had a go at you.'

'But what about—?'

'Don't start again,' Josh warned. 'You'll only make things worse. Go home, Toni. I'll do my own filing.' He smiled a little crookedly. 'I'll finish my spring-cleaning. I'll even wash my own coffee-mugs.'

'You don't need me, then?' Toni asked softly. She held Josh's gaze.

'No. I don't need you.' Josh smiled more confidently. 'Go home. Let's forget about all this. Tomorrow's another day.'

Toni tried to return the smile, failing dismally, but Josh had already turned to pick up the haphazard stack of patient files.

'Sure,' she told him. 'Consider it forgotten.'

But it wasn't forgotten. How could it be? She'd almost confessed her love for Josh. She'd seen the comprehension of what she'd meant in his eyes. She'd seen something else as well. When he'd told her that he hadn't needed her, when he'd told her to go home, his eyes had held another message.

The pathway of communication Toni had seen so clearly yesterday was still there. A firm barrier had been erected on Josh's side but the pathway couldn't be obliterated. If anything, it was more perfectly defined. The journey seemed even more compelling. Toni had to remind herself repeatedly that it was a journey she could no longer contemplate embarking on because it required an invitation she wasn't going to receive.

Josh continued to look preoccupied over the next week. True to his word he made an attempt to tidy up his office, but it was only too easy for Toni to slip back into helpful mode and make the task easier for him. She shifted cartons of journals and other unnecessary clutter into the storeroom, culled the accumulation of toys overflowing the basket Josh kept in his room and arranged the stack of artwork his young patients loved to give him into an attractive wall display. She added a final touch of a small vase of spring blooms to the tidy desk surface after Josh had left on Wednesday evening.

Toni surveyed Josh's consulting room with satisfaction. It had never looked better. The extra task had helped keep her busy enough not to think about herself during working hours. So had fielding the surprisingly large number of responses to the newspaper advertisement for the new receptionist. A visit to Janice Reynolds over the weekend had succeeded in putting Toni's problems into perspective out of working hours, and Toni had also been invited to have dinner with the Reynoldses that evening.

Ben hadn't been at home during Toni's weekend visit. She and Janice had spent time in the garden, as they often did, and between finding seedlings and cuttings for Toni to take home Janice had spoken of her worry about her son.

'He says it's just some virus he's picked up and that Josh is keeping an eye on him, but he's been so distant since he came home. I feel shut out and it hurts.'

'He's been away a long time. Maybe you both need time to adjust.'

'At least I don't have to worry about it being the first stage of Huntington's.' Janice shook her head and sighed. 'It nearly killed me, going through it with Jim, but I had to keep myself together for Ben's sake. Imagine if I'd had to watch it happen to my son when I had no one else to live for.'

Toni simply smiled sympathetically. There was nothing she could think of to say but Janice hadn't expected an answer. She handed Toni a clump of delphinium seedlings.

'There should be some lovely double white ones in that lot.' She smiled at Toni. 'I'm sure Ben will come right. He's going to join the aeroclub this week and get some flying in. That should cheer him up.'

'Is that a good idea at the moment, do you think?' Toni couldn't help sounding doubtful. If Ben's co-ordination and concentration were being affected it could be dangerous.

Janice smiled again and nodded. 'Ben wouldn't fly unless he felt OK. He's an experienced pilot.'

Ben was at home for dinner on Wednesday evening and Janice's prediction seemed to have been correct. He'd taken a small Cessna plane up for the afternoon and had enjoyed himself immensely.

'One of the club pilots came with me, seeing as it was my first time with one of their planes, but I'll be able to get out by myself next week.' He grinned at his mother. 'I might take you for a ride. We could try some aerobatics.'

Janice shuddered. 'I'll pass on the aerobatics but a flight would be fun.'

It was a happy evening, full of reminiscences and hair-raising new stories that Ben hadn't dared put in his letters to his mother.

'She would have been worried sick,' he explained to Toni.

'She would, indeed,' Toni agreed. She watched Ben pick up his spoon as they started their dessert. His hand was trembling slightly and Toni looked away quickly. Ben was happy. His mother was clearly relieved. Any worries Toni had needed to be shelved for the moment.

The worry resurfaced the next morning but there was another matter that needed to be dealt with first. Toni was waiting for Josh to appear in her office.

'Have you heard the news about Bob Granger?' she asked quietly.

Josh frowned as he caught Toni's expression. 'No, what?'

'He died last night. In his sleep. Diane said it was very peaceful.'

Josh nodded briskly. 'That's good.'

Toni's eyes widened at his tone.

'Good that it's over,' Josh amended quickly. 'And good that it was easy. Could have been a lot worse.'

Toni was frowning now. 'He was only forty-three,' she murmured.

'More than some people get.' Josh looked away but Toni stalled his move towards the appointment book. She told him about the previous night's dinner and the visible trembling of Ben's hand.

'Janice has no idea that it might be something serious. She's quite happy that he's flying—she might even go up with him. Don't you think that's a bit dangerous? Maybe she should be told.'

'No,' Josh snapped without hesitation. 'It's Ben's decision. Stay out of it, Toni. It's none of your business.' Turning sharply away to reach for the appointment book, Josh didn't notice the glass of water until he had knocked it over.

'Damn it, Toni!' Josh exploded. 'How many times do you need to be told? That's a bloody stupid place to leave glasses.'

'Sorry.' Toni was rescuing papers. Why was she apologising? It wasn't her fault. The glass had been perfectly well out of harm's way if Josh had been watching what he'd been doing. Maybe he just wanted to distract her from voicing her opinion concerning Ben. Toni opened her mouth, grimly determined to pursue the topic, but the angry stare she was receiving silenced her. Josh wasn't interested in her opinion. Maybe she *was* meddling in a professional situation but the refusal by Josh to even discuss the matter rankled.

Toni was still brooding over the exchange when she knocked on Josh's door later that morning. She opened the door to find him looking far from pleased by the interruption. She noticed that the small vase of flowers she had left on his desk had been pushed aside and was now sitting in a puddle of water, as though the movement had been made with hasty annoyance at its presence.

'What do you want, Swampy?'

Toni's half-smile vanished as she returned Josh's stare. The undertone of irritation in Josh's voice grated. He had already let her know that her opinion regarding a patient was of no interest to him. He hadn't appreciated the feminine touch of flowers on his desk. Her importance she might have had as a practice manager with some potentially urgent query was now being dismissed and the use of the hated nickname negated any importance as a woman. Toni's face tightened.

'For a start, Josh, I would prefer you to use my

name. I have never appreciated being called Swampy.'

Josh looked momentarily disconcerted. 'Really?'

'Really.'

They regarded each other steadily. They both knew she was lying. They both remembered how the nickname had originated—the first day Toni had started at St David's, all those years ago.

The young Dr Cooper had been on the phone to his accountant.

'I've got a receptionist starting today,' he'd said, unaware of Toni standing behind him. 'I'll need her wages to come out of the practice account. Can you work out the tax details?' Josh had listened for a moment and then groaned. 'God, I can't remember. Toni...um. What *is* her surname? Sounded kind of damp. Swamp or something.'

'Marsh,' Toni had supplied, blushing furiously.

Josh had been charmingly embarrassed. It had formed their first bond and had become a private joke between the two of them. They had both appreciated the evidence of communication on a personal level. But not *too* personal. Now Toni was backing off.

'Really,' she said again emphatically. She glared at Josh.

'You've taken your time, letting me know,' Josh said accusingly.

Toni said nothing. He was quite right. How pathetic that she'd allowed the nickname to continue over the years, grateful for the affection it implied. It was a dismal nickname that suddenly seemed to epitomise everything about her. Part of the landscape. Unavoidable and undesirable.

Josh broke the silence. 'Fine,' he said coolly. 'What

would you like me to call you? Miss Marsh?
Antoinette?' He almost winced. Toni's full name had
never crossed his lips before. Now that it had he
looked shocked at its impact.

Toni was equally shocked. She hadn't realised be-
fore how distancing the nickname had been.
Impersonal. Unfeminine. Toni swallowed carefully.
'Toni will do just fine,' she said faintly.

'All right. *Toni.*' The slightly sardonic emphasis
made Toni flinch. She would have preferred a friendly
'Swampy'. 'Was that all you wanted to see me
about?'

'No.' Toni's chin tilted defensively at his dismissive tone. 'I've got several interviews lined up after
5 p.m. for the position of receptionist. I thought you
might like to sit in on them.'

'If I'm available, certainly. Though I think Oliver's
and Sophie's opinions might be of more use.'

'Why?' Toni looked puzzled. 'You'll have to work
with her as well. You are the senior partner here,
Josh.'

Josh looked on the point of saying something, then
shook his head. 'Just let me know when the first one
turns up. I'll be there.'

Toni made her way back to the reception area. God,
Josh looked tired. More than tired. He had a totally
out-of-character air of defeatedness about him. What
was going on? She probably hadn't helped, interfering
in a case that was clearly bothering Josh and then
putting her foot down about her nickname, but it was
time to move on. Sort a few things out. Maybe Josh
needed a bit of a push in the same direction. If he
kept going the way he was, he was likely to make
himself really ill.

The woman who came into the waiting room a few minutes later looked far from really ill.

'Ruby!' Toni greeted her. 'You're looking great. Have you lost some more weight?'

Ruby Murdock nodded modestly. 'I won the prize for member of the month at my weight club. I'm only five kilos off my target weight now.'

'I love the tracksuit.' Toni eyed the powder blue, brushed cotton outfit the older woman was wearing. 'It's even better than the pink one.' Toni leaned over the counter to smile at the small girl clutching Ruby's hand. 'Hi, there, Laura. Would you like a smiley stamp?'

Ruby's grandaughter shook her head and buried her face in the folds of the powder blue track pants.

'She's not feeling very well,' Ruby excused her. 'That's why I popped in. I've just collected her from kindergarten. I wondered if Dr Bennett might be able to see her. Oh!' Ruby pressed her hand to her lips in consternation. 'I suppose she's Dr Spencer now.'

'No.' Toni smiled as she shook her head. 'They decided it would be too confusing when they're working together. Sophie will still be Dr Bennett. She's not here at the moment, though, Ruby. She and Oliver went out to make some house calls.'

Ruby looked disappointed. 'It's probably nothing. It's just that I'm responsible for the children at the moment. My daughter Felicity and her husband have gone to Fiji to have a second honeymoon. I've got all three children for two weeks.'

'That's brave of you, Ruby.'

'It was my idea,' Ruby told her proudly. 'Felicity's done so much for me in the last few years and I don't think all the extra work did much for their marriage.

It's my way of thanking them. I even bought their tickets. I do hope they enjoy themselves. They only left yesterday.'

'They'll be loving it,' Toni assured her. 'Lucky things. Imagine lying on a beach in the sun. Hasn't it got cold again in the last few days?'

Laura tugged at Ruby's hand. 'Nana? I want to go home. I don't feel well.'

Toni eyed the three-year-old's small, flushed face. 'She looks like she could be running a temperature, Ruby. When did she start feeling sick?'

'She was fine this morning,' Ruby told her. 'Though she's got a nasty-looking pimple on her neck. I noticed it when I was brushing her hair. Look.'

Toni looked at the spot. She pursed her lips thoughtfully. 'Has Laura had the chickenpox, Ruby?'

'No, I don't think so.' Ruby looked alarmed. 'Neither have Nathan or Tim. Oh, no!'

'Don't panic.' Toni moved towards the door. 'I'll just go and see if Janet's back from lunch. She'll know.'

Janet wasn't in the staffroom but Toni was pleased to see Josh standing at the bench, eating the sandwich she'd left for him. Her sudden appearance startled him. He coughed and seemed to struggle to swallow his mouthful, finally washing it down with a long slug of coffee. Then he gave Toni a look that suggested it had all been her fault. Toni ignored it.

'Ruby Murdock's in Reception with her granddaughter, Laura. She's looking after the children for two weeks and I think Laura might have chickenpox. I was going to get Janet to have a look but—'

'I'll see her.' Josh dropped the half-eaten sandwich in the rubbish bin.

'I could be wrong,' Toni said anxiously. 'You could have finished your lunch first.'

'I'd had enough,' Josh told her. Then he smiled gently at her dismayed expression. 'And I doubt whether you're wrong, Toni. You've developed an instinct about the people who walk through these doors that I have complete faith in.'

The smile and the compliment flustered Toni. She looked away. 'I'm sure it's what any good receptionist does.'

'Don't you believe it. I've had a lot more experience with receptionists than you have.'

Toni caught his eye. The double meaning was too blatant to ignore. '*That* I do believe!'

Josh laughed. 'That wasn't what I meant, as you well know.' He emptied the rest of his coffee into the sink. 'I've been looking at those CVs from the receptionist applications.' Josh moved towards the door. 'The potential for finding someone else like you is non-existent.'

'It's just a matter of training,' Toni assured him. 'You'll see.'

Toni had short-listed six applicants for the position of receptionist at St David's. Janet was the only staff member who didn't sit in on the interviews. If she had then they would probably have had five differing opinions instead of four.

'I like Gwen Bainbridge,' Oliver said firmly. 'She's got by far the most experience.'

'That's because she's by far the oldest,' Sophie pointed out. 'She's nearly sixty and she struck me as looking rather grumpy.'

'Can't have that,' Josh stated. 'I'm the only one

who's allowed to be grumpy around here. I think Melanie Long is our best bet.'

'That's because she's the best-looking,' Oliver teased. 'You can't resist the sophisticated type.'

'Well, I think we should employ Ricky,' Sophie grinned. 'I like the idea of having a male receptionist.'

Oliver and Josh both groaned. Toni looked defensive. 'You can't specify the sex when you advertise. You have to be seen as an equal opportunities employer. He sounded good on paper.'

'Who do you think would be best, Toni?' Josh sounded serious.

'I liked Sandy Smith,' Toni told them. 'I know she's just a school-leaver but she's bright and keen to learn. She's friendly and confident and communicates well. I think she'd be ideal.'

There was a moment's thoughtful silence. Then Josh nodded. 'I'll go along with that. It's Toni who'll have to train her, and I trust her judgment.'

Oliver and Sophie agreed quickly. They were keen to get home.

'When will she start?' Sophie asked as she buttoned her coat.

'I'll ring her tomorrow,' Toni replied. 'The sooner the better.'

Josh mumbled something inaudible.

Toni raised her eyebrows. 'Is that a problem, Josh?'

'Nothing that a stiff drink and a good night's sleep won't cure,' Josh muttered. 'It's just another change, that's all.'

'A good night's sleep might make a change as well, mate.' Oliver slapped Josh on the back as he followed Sophie out of the staffroom. 'You look like you could use it.'

Josh glared at Oliver's retreating figure. Then he glared at Toni. 'Don't you start,' he warned. 'It's all your fault if I do look tired. Spring-cleaning is exhausting.'

'You finished your office two weeks ago,' Toni informed him. 'At least you *started* two weeks ago. I believe it was me who finished it.'

'And a lovely job you did, too.' Josh's smile was appreciative. 'The flowers were a very nice touch.' His smiled faded, leaving his face rather wistful. 'Doesn't feel quite right, though. It's too tidy. I feel like I'm about to move out.'

'You can mess it up just a little,' Toni said kindly. 'We wouldn't want you to entertain any ideas of moving on. You're as much a part of the furniture around here as I am.'

Josh was staring at her with an odd expression. 'I wish…' He paused, then shook his head, standing up abruptly as he did so. 'Never mind. See you tomorrow, Sw—I mean Toni.'

Toni was still wondering what it was Josh had been tempted to reveal the previous evening when she arrived at St David's the following morning. What *would* Josh wish for? What did he dream of? It seemed unreal to know somebody so well that you could recognise every expression and mood and yet know so little on a more personal level. She had never been allowed close enough. Probably never would be.

Toni sighed heavily. Change the probably to definitely, she told herself. Surely ten years was long enough to be quite sure of that conclusion. Toni glanced at the wall clock as she depressed buttons on the base of the telephone unit. It wasn't strictly necessary to put the phones back from the after hours service before 9 a.m. but Toni usually did so as soon as she arrived. And she could use the distraction of a call or two right now.

One of the doctors was often available early if there was a minor emergency, and Toni was ready with sound advice about the necessity of calling for emergency assistance or whether the problem could wait. She often had a feel about the calls that came early, and she knew as soon as she picked up the phone on that Friday morning that this call was different.

Oliver and Sophie came in a minute later as Toni sat, tears rolling unchecked down her face. Her hand still clutched the telephone receiver. It was shaking noticeably.

'My God, Toni!' Oliver dropped his bag as he rushed to her side. 'What's happened?'

'It's Josh.' Toni found it difficult to force the words past her stiff lips. 'He's been in a car accident.'

CHAPTER FIVE

'A CAR accident!' Sophie went nearly as pale as Toni. 'Oh, God! Is he hurt?'

Toni shook her head hard. 'He says he isn't but...but...' A sob broke through. 'He *might* have been.'

Oliver and Sophie exchanged meaningful glances. Sophie put her arm around Toni. 'It'll be all right,' she said reassuringly.

'Where is he?' Oliver demanded. 'And what happened?'

'He's on Centaurus Road, at the roundabout. He said he'll probably be late. He—' Toni stopped suddenly. They could all hear the distant wail of a siren. 'You don't think that's...?'

Oliver smiled and shook his head. 'If he rang to say he'll be late I don't think he'll need an ambulance. It's only two minutes' drive away. I'll go and have a look.' He raised his eyebrows questioningly. 'Would you like to come with me, Toni?'

Toni laughed shakily. 'Oh, no! He wouldn't want me turning up. I don't know why I'm reacting like this, really.'

Sophie and Oliver exchanged glances again, this time accompanied by knowing smiles.

'It's a bit of a shock,' Sophie offered.

'Yes, that's it.' Toni's voice gathered strength. 'It was just a bit of a shock.'

'Let's have a cup of tea,' Sophie suggested. She

nodded at Oliver. 'Make sure Josh gets a check-up if he needs it. We women will hold the fort here.'

They expected the men to be a long time but Oliver's car rolled back into the car park only twenty minutes later. They could hear Josh grumbling before he even came inside.

'It's nothing. For heaven's sake, Oliver. Give me a break.'

'You might have given yourself one,' Oliver countered. 'At least let me have a look at that bump on your head.'

Toni was staring, transfixed. Josh looked pale, shaken and…angry. He had a purple-edged lump the size of a golf ball on his forehead. He also had blood on his shirt.

'I'll get some ice,' Toni stated calmly. 'Take him into the side room, Oliver. He can lie down for a while.'

'I do not need to lie down,' Josh said irritably. 'I'm not an invalid. I'm going into my room. I'd like some black coffee, please, Toni. And you can send my first patient in.' Josh stalked off.

Toni looked at Oliver appealingly. He shook his head and shrugged.

'I don't think he's got a concussion,' he answered Toni's mute appeal. 'But he's pretty fed up.'

'What happened?' Sophie asked. 'Was it Josh's fault?'

'No.' Oliver chuckled wryly. 'A kitten ran out on the road in front of him, although, knowing Josh, he was probably going too fast for the frosty conditions. Poor chap wrote off the front half of his precious car when he cleaned up a rubbish bin and then went into a lamppost, trying to avoid hitting the animal.'

'Did he? Avoid the kitten, I mean.'

'Not quite. It got trapped between the rubbish bin and the lamppost. That was how Josh hurt his head, trying to extricate it. The blood's not all his. He'd just got the kitten out when I arrived.' Oliver smiled at the expressions of his audience. 'It's OK. Didn't seem too badly hurt. We dropped it off at the vet on our way back. It had a few cuts and probably a broken leg.' Oliver chuckled again. 'And it bit Josh.'

Somehow the added injury to the insult of damaging Josh's car seemed to lessen the fright they'd all had. The laughter was a little inappropriate but a necessary release. Josh's door flew open.

'When you've all quite finished having a good laugh at my expense—and I might add that the expense will undoubtedly be horrendous—perhaps we could all get on with the business of running a medical centre.' Josh glared at them. 'Where the hell's Janet? Is she late *again*?' He didn't bother waiting for a response. 'I thought you were getting me some coffee, Toni.'

Toni added two spoons of sugar to the black coffee. She also got an ice pack out of the freezer and collected a packet of Panadol tablets from the treatment room. She found Josh sitting at his desk. He was finishing a phone call as she entered.

'At least the insurance company was more sympathetic.' Josh scowled at the items Toni deposited on his desk. 'I only wanted the coffee,' he said ungraciously.

'You should be grateful someone cares about you,' Toni snapped. 'For goodness sake, Josh. You could have been really hurt.' She felt tears gather again and blinked furiously.

Josh's scowl faded. 'Sorry.' His smile was concil-
iatory. 'I don't deserve to have you care, do I?'

'No.' Toni set down the coffee mug beside the
packet of tablets. She looked at Josh cautiously.
'You're not, are you?'

'Not what?'

'Really hurt.' Toni's voice wobbled slightly.

Josh reached for his coffee-mug and his fingers
brushed Toni's. He grasped her hand and gave it a
reassuring squeeze. 'I'm not hurt at all. Apart from
my pride. It's the first accident I've ever had. And
then I was stupid enough to bang my head on the
lamppost while I was trying to see whether I'd
squashed the damned cat.'

Toni was staring at his hand. If he was unhurt, why
was his hand trembling? Or was it hers? Josh saw the
direction of her gaze and snatched his hand away before she could be sure. The reassurance in his voice
was gone.

'I'll use the ice pack if it'll make you happy,' he
growled. 'Now just go away and let me get on with
some work. I'm sure you've got more than enough to
do yourself.'

Josh was right. Patients had accumulated in the
waiting area. Ruby Murdock was back again. She had
two miserable-looking small boys with her. Laura sat
on her knee, her face now covered with spots. Ruby
smiled bravely at Toni.

'I've got them all off school,' she said. 'The boys
haven't got any spots yet but they're not well. And
poor Laura's terribly itchy. I hope Dr Bennett can
help.'

'I'm sure she can.' Toni smiled sympathetically at
the prospect of the difficult week Ruby had ahead of

her. 'Bring them all down to Sophie's room, Ruby.'
Toni led the way. 'She'll be with you in just a minute.'

Toni had intended to ring Sandy Smith first thing
to let her know she'd been successful in her bid for
the position as receptionist but she was flat out for
the next half-hour and there was still no sign of any
let-up.

'Dr Cooper wants to refer me to a dermatologist,'
the elderly woman at the counter was explaining to
Toni. 'He suggested Dr Amberley. I want to go privately. I've got insurance.'

'That's fine, Mrs Batchelor. Would you like me to
make an appointment for you now?'

'Oh, yes, please, dear. It's driving me crazy.' She
leaned over the counter and lowered her voice. 'I'm
so *itchy*. And it's a place you just can't scratch. Not
in public, anyway.'

Toni's sympathetic smile was getting well used today. She nodded at the young man standing behind
Mrs Batchelor, waiting to pay for his visit. 'Be with
you in a moment, Terry. You'll need to fill in an ACC
form.' She handed the paper over and then focused
her attention on the specialist phone list on the wall.
She dialed the number for Dr Amberley's clinic.

'What has poor Dr Cooper done to his head?' Mrs
Batchelor asked.

'He had a bit of a bump this morning. He was
saving a kitten.' Toni uncovered the mouthpiece of
the telephone. 'Michelle? Hi. It's Toni—St David's
Medical Centre. I need an appointment with Dr
Amberley, please, as soon as possible.' She raised her
eyebrows enquiringly at Mrs Batchelor who nodded
vigorously.

'Isn't that just like Dr Cooper,' her patient said admiringly to the young man beside her. '*Such* a nice man.'

Terry was frowning at the form in front of him on the counter.

'They can fit you in next Wednesday, Mrs Batchelor. Two p.m.?'

'Oh, no, dear. That wouldn't do at all, I'm afraid. I play mah-jong on Wednesday afternoons.'

'What do I put in here?' Terry demanded. 'I don't really have to say exactly how I hurt my back, do I?'

Sophie swooped in to collect a new patient file. Ruby Murdock ushered her three grandchildren towards the toy box and then joined the end of the queue at the counter.

A toddler who had been triumphantly balancing on his feet holding onto the magazine rack, slipped, bumped his head and started wailing. Toni gripped the phone harder. 'What about Thursday at 11 a.m., Mrs Batchelor?'

'Let me think, dear.' Mrs Batchelor focused on a distant point somewhere over Toni's shoulder. 'I think that might be all right. Where exactly is Dr Amberley's clinic?'

'Merivale.'

'Ooh! That's a long way away. I don't drive, you know.'

The toddler refused to be pacified by his embarrassed mother. The shrieking increased in volume. Ruby Murdock was looking over Terry's shoulder.

'How *did* you hurt your back, love?'

Terry's eyes widened at the sight of the luminous pink track suit. Then he grinned. 'Sex,' he told Ruby. 'In the shower. I slipped.'

'Well. I never!' Ruby's astonished expression became a knowing smile. 'I don't suppose you *do* want to put that on the compensation form.'

Toni hung up the phone. 'Just put that you slipped in the shower,' she advised Terry. 'Mrs Batchelor? I've written your appointment time on this card. If you want to change it you can ring the clinic yourself. Now, that will be twenty-five dollars for this morning's appointment.'

'Oh? Dr Cooper said there'd be no charge.'

'Really?' Toni had seen the flicker of interest in Ruby's face. No doubt she would be asking for an appointment with the generous Dr Cooper next time. She nodded and then turned to Terry.

'Did Dr Spencer give you a medical certificate to say how long you'd need to be off work?'

'He said I'd need a week off. I have to do a lot of lifting.'

'Has he given you a note?'

'No.'

'I'd better check on that.' Toni ducked out of the office. She poked her head into the treatment room. Janet was tickling a small baby who lay in the bowl of the scales.

'Janet, could you grab the phone, please?' Toni found Oliver standing in the kitchen with Sophie. They were both drinking coffee. 'Oliver, did you write a certificate for Terry?'

'It's on my desk. Sorry, Toni.' Oliver turned back to Sophie with a broad grin. 'That reminds me. I think we'd better cross the shower off the list. Or at least be very careful what we do with the soap...'

Toni almost cannoned into Josh as she tried to leave the kitchen.

'It's bloody chaos out there, Toni. I think you could arrange a better time to have a morning teabreak.'

Toni gave him a dirty look but said nothing.

'And can't you shut that infernal racket up? Give the kid a lollipop or something.'

'He's your patient,' Toni responded sharply. 'Perhaps you'd like to see him now?'

'I've got enough of a headache, thanks. Send him in when he's stopped screeching.' Josh brushed past Toni. 'I'm going to have another coffee.'

The information that Josh was suffering from a headache failed to arouse any fresh sympathy in Toni. She had one herself. Snatching Terry's certificate off Oliver's desk, Toni marched back into her office. By the time she'd dealt with both Terry and Ruby, the toddler had subsided into loud hiccups. His mother was eyeing the bump on his forehead anxiously. Toni took them down to Josh's room.

'Guess what?' she said to the small boy. 'Dr Cooper's got a bump just like yours.'

Sophie was now examining the baby in the treatment room. Janet came into the office with a small cool box.

'These samples need to go to the lab. Ross should be here in a minute.' Janet sighed heavily. 'It's one of those days, isn't it?'

'You're telling me,' Toni agreed wearily. 'They all seem to be at the moment. Maybe it's the weather. Too cold. And when it's not frosty, it's raining.'

'Is Josh all right? Sounds like he just about wrote off his car and he's in a filthy mood. He's already had a go at me this morning.'

'He's fine. Just as bad-tempered as usual. He's curing himself with black coffee. What did he have a go at you about?'

'Oh, some drugs he claimed to have told me to order last week, including narcotics. We're pretty low but it was the first I'd heard about it. I faxed through the requisition immediately but Josh wasn't happy.'

'He hasn't been happy for weeks,' Toni muttered. 'In fact, the morale around this place has slipped considerably.'

Janet grinned. 'Oliver and Sophie seem pretty happy.'

'They probably haven't noticed a thing. They're firmly ensconced on cloud nine.' Toni's breath came out in a long sigh. 'I suppose it's my morale that's really slipped. I can't seem to get on top of things and I seem to be in the firing line of Josh Cooper's moods no matter which way I turn.'

'It'll get better when we get the new receptionist.' Janet raised her eyebrows. 'How did the interviews go? Did you make a decision?'

Toni nodded. 'Yes. A Sandy Smith. She's young and keen. Thanks for reminding me, Toni. I've got to ring and let her know she's got the job.' Toni reached for a manila folder on her desk. 'Her number should be on her CV.'

'Is she going to be full time?'

'Not initially. Probably just afternoons, though we can be flexible. She does a few babysitting jobs at present. We might be able to work around that. Hopefully it will turn into a full-time position for her.' Toni paused and looked thoughtful. She shot Janet a sideways glance. 'Do you know, Jan, when I've got young Sandy trained up I might just start looking for another job myself.'

Janet's eyes widened in consternation. 'Because of Josh?'

Toni nodded. 'He's becoming impossible to work for. I used to love this job but just lately I've wished I could turn the clock back ten years. I wish I'd never set foot in the door.'

The foot that came through the office door at that moment belonged to Josh. Toni flushed, wondering how much of the conversation he'd overheard. Then she raised her chin defiantly. It was true. Josh *was* becoming impossible to work for, although not simply because of his moodiness. The idea of going somewhere else had been percolating ever since that staff meeting had prompted it. A new job. A new start.

Josh was staring at Toni. Janet edged out of the office behind him. 'You can't be serious,' he said quietly.

'Can't I?'

'We're a team, Toni. I couldn't manage without you.'

'Yes, you could.' Toni looked away. 'I'll be able to train Sandy up in no time at all. She might even take care of your dry cleaning and putting off your ex-girlfriends. I should add it into the job description.'

'But could you add in being a friend?' Josh's expression was troubled. 'Being able to put up with the bad temper and understand that it doesn't lessen how much the support is appreciated?'

'Nobody would take on a job with that description.' Toni had to smile. She could see the real Josh for the first time in weeks. The tug at her loyalty was too strong to ignore.

'Exactly.' Josh still looked troubled. 'I'm sorry, Toni. I've been making life difficult for you. I've decided it's my lifestyle to blame. I'm too old to keep it up and I'm going to turn over a new leaf.' He smiled appealingly. 'I'll be nice, I promise. Especially to you.'

The ringing phone jarred the melting effect Josh's smile was having.

'St David's Medical Centre, Toni speaking.' She knew Josh was still watching her. 'Hello, Mr Collins. How are you this week? No…really? Um, that sounds a bit serious. I'll see if Dr Cooper can fit you in this afternoon.' The look Toni directed at Josh was challenging.

He started to shake his head but then grinned sheepishly. Toni glanced at the appointment book. 'Two forty-five, Mr Collins. Just try and rest until then.' She filled in the slot. 'Chest pains, palpitations, sweating and nausea,' she informed Josh.

'Surprise, surprise,' Josh murmured. 'It's the flavour of the month. He's been reading up on the Reader's Digest guide to heart problems.'

'One of these days he's going to have something genuine wrong with him,' Toni warned.

'As long as it doesn't arrive in a jam jar.' Josh's smile held a silent plea, an appeal to Toni to consider their history together. The dozens of patients they both knew so well—like Mr Collins, who invariably came to his appointments armed with specimens of dubious medical interest. The bond that Josh and Toni shared epitomised the thread of continuity and loyalty that held St David's together. Toni's nod was almost imperceptible, her gentle smile an acknowledgment of a bond that couldn't be lightly discarded.

Josh's face relaxed. His smile now held a different appeal. 'Could you ring the vet for me, please, Toni?

If you get the time, that is,' he added hastily. 'I'd just like to know whether that damned cat's survived.'

The kitten had survived but any pleasure in the news was quickly forgotten.

'I've just had a call from Janice Reynolds,' Toni informed Josh quietly. 'Ben went flying this morning. He was planning to go to the West Coast. Janice was planning to go with him but changed her mind.' Toni's face twisted anxiously. 'Ben was due to arrive there two hours ago but nobody's heard anything. They've just reported him missing.'

Josh eyed Toni silently.

'You spoke to him yesterday, didn't you, Josh?' Toni queried. 'How did he seem?'

'Not great,' Josh admitted reluctantly. 'He'd had a bit of an incident eating lunch. Fortunately Janice was out.'

'What sort of incident?'

'He…uh…had trouble swallowing his food. Ended up vomiting.'

'Oh, God,' Toni breathed. 'Just like his father.'

Josh's expression was grim. 'Don't jump to conclusions, Toni. He would hardly have invited his mother along on the trip if he wasn't planning to come back. We don't know what's happened yet.'

It took most of the weekend to locate the wreckage of Ben Reynolds's plane and to retrieve his body. Toni spent the weekend with Janice, the misery of the situation deepened by having to keep the information about Ben's state of health to herself.

Josh found her in the staffroom of St David's early on Monday morning.

'You look dreadful,' he said with concern.

'You don't look so great yourself.' Toni smiled shakily through the last of her recent bout of tears.

'How's Janice?'

'Devastated. I've told her I'll send you round to see her this morning. I think she'll need something to help her get through the next few days.'

Josh nodded. 'I'll go first thing if you can juggle the appointments.'

'Will you tell her?' Toni didn't need to elaborate on what they both knew was probably the truth about Ben's accident.

'No.'

Toni looked away from the pain in Josh's expression. 'It might be easier for her to come to terms with Ben's death if she knows—'

'If she knows how much worse it could have been if he'd lived?' Josh interrupted dryly. He shook his head. 'Ben wanted to spare her the knowledge that he'd inherited Huntington's. Do we have the right to take that away from him?'

'I suppose not,' Toni said reluctantly.

Josh touched her arm softly. 'Do you think it would be easier for Janice to accept if she knew it wasn't an accident? If she knew that Ben had kept his fears to himself for all those years?'

'I guess she might feel hurt that she'd been shut out. She might even blame herself.'

'It's hard to accept the death of anyone you love,' Josh said gently. 'Suicide can be much harder to accept than an accident. It's the ultimate rejection, isn't it?'

'We don't know for sure that it wasn't an accident,' Toni suggested hesitantly.

'No.'

'And we don't know for sure that Ben did have Huntington's.'

'No, we don't,' Josh agreed somberly. 'And the professional confidentiality of what we do know has to be treated with respect. By both of us.'

The bond between them seemed stronger than ever. They were a team—she and Josh. Toni nodded slowly.

'Will you come to the funeral service tomorrow?'

Josh looked away but not before Toni realised how difficult the prospect was for him. 'Are you going?' he asked tightly.

'Of course.'

Josh cleared his throat and returned his gaze to Toni. 'Then we'll go together,' he offered. 'If that's OK with you.'

'I'd like that.' Toni's smile felt rusty. 'Thanks, Josh.'

CHAPTER SIX

ATTENDING a funeral service for a patient was fortunately a rare occurrence for the staff at St David's.

Josh blamed his red eyes and stuffy nose on the cold he'd come down with, but his hand was locked tightly with Toni's as they sat through the service. The cold might well have been genuine but Josh was suffering more than physically. Toni found his unspoken distress unsettling. Ben had been his patient for only a very short period of time. Even given the instant rapport the two men had discovered, the impact of Ben's death on Josh seemed more than a professional relationship could account for. Did Josh feel there was more he could, or should, have done? Was he as troubled as Toni was by the secret they shared?

Janice was grateful for their presence. She was trying very hard to keep herself under control.

'At least we had a little time together again,' she told Josh and Toni as they took their turn to offer their condolences. 'This could have happened any time in the last ten years—anywhere in the world. And he was so happy for the last few days.'

'It was a lovely evening we had together on Wednesday,' Toni agreed. 'Ben did seem very happy.'

'He told me that it was a difficult decision to make but he'd realised it was the right one.'

Toni's glance flicked towards Josh.

'What decision was that, Janice?' Josh's tone was guarded.

Janice looked momentarily bewildered, as though she was trying to remember. 'To come home, I suppose,' she said slowly. 'To stop living life in the fast lane.'

'And to spend some time with his mum.' Toni reached forward to hug Janice. 'I'm just so sorry you didn't have longer, Janice. Much, much longer.'

Fresh tears rolled down the older woman's cheeks. 'Maybe people like Ben can't ever settle down. They throw themselves at life until it finally catches up with them.'

Toni was silent during the drive back to St David's. People like Ben. Like Josh. How many times had Josh been attracted to dangerous pursuits? Over the years he'd tried skydiving, scuba-diving and cross-country skiing. He drove fast cars and only recently had talked of a desire to learn to fly himself. Was he destined never to settle down as well? Was that why his relationships with women were intense but short-lived? Why someone like Toni was a frightening prospect?

Josh's cold had worsened by the next day. He was blowing his nose and looking miserable when Toni produced a fresh box of tissues and some paracetamol for him. She told him about the call from the veterinary clinic she'd just received. The kitten was ready to go home but no one had claimed it. There was also an outstanding bill of $300 for the surgery to the broken leg.

Josh's look of misery deepened.

'Three hundred dollars? What did they do, set the leg in a gold-plated cast?'

Toni smiled, appreciative of Josh's attempt at humour when he was obviously feeling lousy. The atmosphere between them was still subdued in the wake of Ben's funeral, and the reminder of Josh's accident was sobering. The bruise on his forehead had almost gone but the aftermath of the incident was clearly going to last much longer. His car would be off the road for weeks and the only replacement vehicle the panel-beating company had had available was a rather battered old van which was hardly Josh's usual style.

'At least I didn't kill it.' Josh sighed. 'I thought it was probably someone's treasured pet.'

'Apparently not.' Toni had had a long chat to the veterinary nurse. 'They said it's really sweet. It's a boy—about four months old, but very undernourished. They've vaccinated and wormed him but he's in desperate need of a home.'

'Not with me, he isn't.' Josh blew his nose again vigorously. 'I've got a penthouse apartment and the lease specifies no animals.' He looked at Toni a little blearily. 'Why don't you take it? One more won't make any difference.'

'Oh, no!' Toni shook her head. 'I have enough trouble trying to keep my lot honest. The last thing they need is an apprentice.'

'Maybe Janet would like a kitten. I'm sure the boys would approve.'

'There's always the SPCA. Would you like me to ring them for you?'

'No.' Josh shook his head wearily. 'I created this problem. For once, I'll sort it out myself.' He smiled valiantly at Toni. 'See? I really am turning over a new leaf.'

'Come and have some lunch first,' Toni suggested. 'Things are quiet and Sandy can cope for a bit.'

'How's it going? I'm afraid I haven't been very sociable. I didn't want to give the poor girl my cold on her first day.'

'She's great,' Toni said confidently. 'Picking things up fast.' Toni smiled at Josh. Training Sandy was a good distraction from the bleak mood Ben's funeral had left her with. Maybe the kitten would provide Josh with a similar distraction. Once in the staffroom, Toni placed a sandwich beside Josh's mug of coffee. Chicken salad had always been a favourite of his. Josh was talking earnestly to Janet but his practice nurse didn't seem impressed with the idea of adopting a kitten.

'The boys would love it,' Josh said encouragingly.

'The boys love anything with four legs and fur,' Janet agreed, 'but they've set their hearts on a dog. It's all I hear about these days.'

'Give them a kitten instead,' Josh advised. 'You don't have to worry about leaving it at home alone while you're working. And they're much cheaper to keep.'

'Sure are.' Oliver grinned. 'Only three hundred dollars for a broken leg.'

Toni eyed the sandwich Josh was fiddling with. He hadn't even unwrapped it.

'This kitten's an orphan,' Josh told Janet sadly. 'And it's really cute.'

'I thought it bit you.' Sophie had finished her lunch quickly and was eyeing the muffin Oliver had started on.

'It was hurt. And scared,' Josh said defensively. He caught Toni's eye suddenly. 'I'd do the same myself.'

Josh's gaze suggested he was defending more than the kitten, and Toni frowned slightly. What was the unspoken message? And why did it stir up such a distinct feeling of disquiet?

The others hadn't noticed anything. Oliver and Sophie were laughing as they listened to Janet.

'And after the rabbit escaped, there were the goldfish. They got flushed down the loo. By mistake, so Adam claimed. They were very sad about it.'

'Not half as sad as the goldfish, I'll bet,' Oliver said, chuckling.

'And then there was the guinea pig,' Janet said in a hollow tone. 'Wilbur. The boys loved Wilbur.'

'And?' Sophie prompted. She took the other half of the muffin off Oliver's plate.

'Hey! That's my lunch,' Oliver protested.

'They loved Wilbur so much they made him a feast,' Janet continued. 'Bits of chopped-up carrot and apple. Grass. Even a corn cob. They spent all morning collecting it and arranging it on a platter.'

'I'm still hungry,' Oliver said plaintively.

'So was Wilbur.' Janet grinned. 'He ate the lot. Unfortunately the boys had decorated the feast with buttercups.'

'Have my sandwich,' Josh offered, pushing it towards Oliver.

'Buttercups are deadly to guinea pigs,' Janet finished sadly. 'Poor Wilbur never stood a chance.'

'Maybe you could turn the hutch into a cat box,' Josh suggested. 'It's a pretty small kitten.'

'No way,' Janet said firmly. 'You saved its life, Josh. You'll have to keep it.'

Sandy came into the staffroom, looking for Toni.

'There's a courier here. He's got some drug supplies and says we have to sign for them. Do I do that?'

'No, I'd better take care of that, Sandy. There'll be some samples to go back with him to the lab as well. See if there's a plastic bag with vacutubes in Janet's room.'

'There is,' Janet confirmed. 'I'll show you, Sandy. I always put them beside the autoclave.'

Sandy's eyes widened. 'What's that?'

'The steriliser. It looks like a large bread bin.' Janet was leading the way. Both Sandy and Toni followed. 'There's often something in the fridge as well.'

Toni introduced Sandy to Ross, the courier. 'You're lucky to get a job here,' Ross congratulated Sandy. 'How's it going?'

'I've only just started,' Sandy replied. 'I love it but I've got an awful lot to learn.'

'You'll get there,' Ross assured her. He grinned at Toni. 'You'll be able to put your feet up soon. Or take a nice, long holiday.'

'Something like that,' Toni murmured. She signed for the drugs and handed over the samples. 'Thanks, Ross. We'll see you later.'

Toni opened up the small carton of drug supplies. 'There are some narcotic supplies in here,' she told Sandy. 'We don't keep very much on the premises and they need to go in the floor safe. See that loose bit of carpet over there?'

Sandy nodded enthusiastically.

'Lift it up. I'll tell you the combination and you can open the safe. You'll need to learn it off by heart because we don't keep it written down.'

'Cool!' Sandy was already kneeling on the floor. 'I've never cracked a safe before.'

Toni smiled at her eager face. Sandy was only eighteen, very cheerful and willing to try anything. Ross was right. It wouldn't take her long to get to grips with her new job and she was clearly enjoying herself. Everything was new and often a surprise.

It wasn't just Sandy who was surprised by the box left on the counter at lunchtime early the following week. Sandy opened it.

'Oh, look!' she gasped. 'It's a kitten! Isn't it gorgeous?' She lifted out the undersized black kitten and exclaimed again at the cast on its leg. 'It's hurt,' she told Toni in horror. Then her face creased with confusion. 'But we don't treat animals here, do we?'

'Not usually.' Toni touched the kitten's silky head. The tiny animal pushed against her hand and started purring loudly. 'I think Dr Cooper might know something about this patient.' Toni took the silky black bundle from Sandy and led the way to the staffroom where Josh was still lingering over his coffee, conversing with Oliver.

'Did you arrange a delivery?' The kitten was trying to stand up in Toni's arms to rub its chin against her face. Toni had to smile at the volume of the purr.

'I couldn't have it sent to the SPCA,' Josh mumbled. 'It might have been put down.'

Oliver was grinning. 'That would have been a bit of a waste of three hundred dollars.'

'Exactly.' Josh eyed the kitten. 'It *is* quite cute, isn't it?'

'I thought you couldn't keep pets in your apartment,' Toni reminded him.

'I can't.' Josh cleared his throat. 'Hey, Sandy, would you like a kitten?'

'I'd love one but I'm living at home and Mum gets terrible asthma from cats.'

Josh looked disappointed but then raised one eyebrow. 'It could stay here for a while. Maybe one of our patients will take pity on it and give it a home.'

'It could live here,' Sandy suggested eagerly. 'If you gave it a bed and a dirt box.'

'I don't think so,' Josh said hurriedly. 'It would probably be breaking some health regulation. Especially a dirt box.'

'You could put a cat door in the French windows, then,' Sandy suggested.

'It could be taught to stay out of the treatment room,' Toni put in. 'I think it's a great idea. We're a family health centre not a hospital. Lots of rest homes and so on have a cat. And this wee chap's so friendly. He'd probably love to hang out in the waiting room.'

'Pets are very therapeutic.' Oliver was obviously intrigued by the notion. 'We could do a study and see if the complaints of being kept waiting drop off.'

Toni took a step forward and deposited the kitten on Josh's lap. 'You saved his life,' she announced. 'It's your call, Josh.'

Oliver watched, a broad grin on his face. Sandy had an imploring expression on her face. Toni found she had to swallow carefully as she saw the softening of Josh's face, the gentle touch as he tickled the kitten under its chin. The appreciative response made Oliver chuckle.

'Sounds like an outboard motor.'

'Outboard!' Sandy exclaimed. 'What a cool name! Can we keep him, Dr Cooper? *Please?*'

Josh sighed. 'I suppose so. For the moment, anyway. It'll be your job to look after him, Sandy, and keep him out of mischief.'

'I'll find a box and an old towel for a bed. And I can buy some cat food when I go down to the bank.' Sandy reached happily for the kitten. 'Come on, Outboard.'

'We'd better sort out a dirt box first. Leave him here for now, Sandy,' Toni instructed. 'We've got some work to get on with for now.'

Outboard settled into the staffroom instantly, spending his time asleep unless he had company. Toni envied him his hours of repose. It was more tiring than she'd expected, training her assistant. Many efforts by the new receptionist had to be corrected or redone and Toni had to be vigilant in checking. The appointment book had lost its usual neatness as multiple entries were changed, sometimes more than once.

'That's why I always use a pencil,' Toni explained. 'It's much easier to change things and still keep them clear.'

'I'm sorry about Mrs Harrison,' Sandy said anxiously. 'She didn't sound as if it was anything urgent and the doctors were all fully booked for today.'

'Urgent appointments always get squeezed in.' Toni smiled reassuringly at Sandy. 'Don't worry. You weren't to know about Eileen Harrison. I know she makes things sound trivial but she's been coming here for years. Eileen doesn't ring unless there's something seriously wrong. She's over ninety and has heart failure but she usually stays quite active and doesn't like to think she's a bother to anyone.'

Another entry had to be rubbed out. 'You'll need to ring John Drummond back and change this appointment, Sandy. It's for minor surgery and needs a double appointment time. We usually try and keep those for a Thursday or Friday morning.'

'Oh.' Sandy chewed her lip. 'Will his phone number be on the computer file?'

'Yes. See if you can find it by yourself.'

Sandy looked happier when she'd completed her task successfully. 'I've put him down for next Friday. A half-hour appointment,' she told Toni.

'Great.'

'Why have these Wednesday afternoon times got a line through them?'

'That's Sophie's column. She's still doing her GP training and has tutorial or workshop sessions at the hospital on Wednesday afternoons. We try and keep Thursday afternoons free for her as well for a study period. She's got her exams coming up in October.'

'What about house calls? Do they need a double appointment time, too?'

'At least.' Toni nodded. 'We try and keep them to a minimum and only within a certain area. See the circle on the map up there?' Toni pointed to the street map of Christchurch pinned to the wall.

'How will I know who really needs them?'

'Rest-home patients are automatically house calls. So are our terminally ill patients. You'll get to know the names after a while. I'll make a list for you in the meantime. Any calls you're not sure about, hand over to me. Some people can be quite demanding but house calls aren't a standard service for GPs any more.'

'I'll never be able to do this job as well as you can, Toni. You know so much about everything.'

'I've had plenty of time to learn.' Toni smiled wryly. 'Don't worry. It'll all get easier very quickly.'

Sandy Smith's learning curve was well under way. By the following week, Toni found the pressure on herself easing noticeably. Sandy had taken over many of the time-consuming, routine tasks like greeting patients, taking payment for accounts and the daily trip to the local shopping centre to do the banking and other messages. She even took over collecting the lunch supplies at the bakery and had learned everybody's favourites.

Not that Josh was eating much. He began to look better as the symptoms of his cold subsided but he was still too pale and definitely subdued. Toni wondered whether it had something to do with the long consultations he'd had with Janice Reynolds on two occasions over the last week. She knew Janice had finally persuaded him to prescribe her a course of antidepressants.

'I just need something to get me through the next month or two,' Janice had explained apologetically to Toni. 'Then I'll be all right.'

'I know you will,' Toni had responded gently. 'It takes time, Janice.'

Josh was also confident that Janice would be able to cope. 'I've referred her to a professional counsellor,' he told Toni. 'I'm not so good at situations like this.'

'That's not true,' Toni protested. 'You understand what people are going through very well.'

'Too well,' Josh grunted. 'That's the problem.' He fiddled with the sandwich Toni had given him. 'It's too hard on those left behind,' he said suddenly, pushing the sandwich away. 'Thank goodness I haven't got a family. Especially a wife or kids. Imagine how many more people would have been devastated if Ben had decided to add those into his life.' Josh gave Toni an odd smile. 'Nobody's going to crash too badly if I pop off.'

'That's a terrible attitude to have!' Toni exclaimed.

Josh narrowed his eyes at her tone. 'Why?'

'It's isolationist. Selfish.'

'Selfish! Don't you think it might have been a sacrifice on Ben's part to stay alone? He wanted to spare his mother the anguish of losing him for as long as possible. Maybe he had some woman he was deeply in love with but he never embarked on the relationship to spare her the same grief.'

'Well, if she was in love with him as well, it would have been very cruel.'

Josh blinked. 'Surely it would have been cruel to offer her something that could have no future.'

Toni shook her head. 'I disagree, Josh. It would have been more cruel to let her go through life thinking he hadn't been aware of her love or hadn't felt the same way about her.' Toni sighed. 'And I think Ben missed out, too. He probably thought he was getting the best life had to offer with his adventurous lifestyle and never settling in one place or with one relationship, but *I* reckon he bypassed the most important thing of all. He missed out on really getting the best life has to offer.'

Josh was silent. He appeared to be giving serious consideration to Toni's opinion. Too serious. She was disturbed by the haunted expression in his dark eyes. This was a hypothetical discussion. Wasn't it? What was it about the case of Ben Reynolds that had affected Josh so deeply? It was out of character for him to be so subdued, and not all of it could be attributed to the nasty virus he'd had. The fact that he'd ignored his lunch again was more like Josh. Toni eyed the sandwich.

'You seem to be living on black coffee around here. It's not healthy, Josh.'

Toni expected a rebuke for nagging him. She would have welcomed one, in fact, as an indication that things were getting back to normal. But Josh gave her a half-hearted smile that made Toni stare. She glanced down at the movement of Josh's hand as he stroked Outboard. Maybe it was the unsettling domesticity of the small, black cat ensconced on his lap that made Josh appear to be behaving oddly. The image was dispelled when Josh spoke again, however.

'I hate cooking,' he admitted. 'My idea of meal preparation is a lengthy perusal of a menu. Eating's the interesting bit. Everything else is too slow. Boring.'

Toni had to laugh at his expression of distaste. 'Haven't you ever heard that getting there is half the fun?'

Josh's grin was much more like his usual style. 'I've heard it. I've just never believed it.'

'I haven't booked a restaurant table for you since Oliver's and Sophie's wedding. That's over a month ago now.'

'I haven't been to a restaurant since then.'

'So what have you been eating?'

Josh shrugged. 'Whatever's in the cupboard. Soup. Baked beans. It's too dull to try and remember.'

'No wonder it's taken so long to shake that cold off. And I'm not surprised you're losing weight and looking terrible.' Toni put her chin down and gave

Josh a stern look. 'Come around to my house. Tonight. Seven o'clock.'

Josh's eyebrows shot up. 'Are you offering to cook for me?'

'No.' Toni kept her tone firm. 'I'm offering you a cooking lesson. A new experience. You might even find it tastes better when it's taken some time to prepare.'

What *had* she done?

Toni watched Outboard limp rapidly across the staffroom floor, having been abandoned gently by Josh. She reached down and scooped up the kitten for a moment, enjoying the affectionate rub of the tiny black head and the crescendo of purrs. Outboard had added considerably to the atmosphere of St David's in a way no one had anticipated.

The patients loved it when he appeared in the waiting room. Children were much keener to go to the doctor and Toni had seen some of their elderly, lonely patients smiling with real pleasure at a chance to touch the friendly animal. It gave St David's a homely atmosphere and Toni was in need of the comfort it could offer. Had she really invited Josh for dinner? At her home?

When he'd accepted the invitation she'd experienced a glow of delight. The pleasure of having an offering accepted, a pleasure that could only be that intense when the acceptance was deeply significant. The delight had been short-lived, however. The pleasure was quickly replaced by an emotion she hadn't previously associated with her interactions with Josh Cooper. Toni identified the emotion as fear. Or, at least, a nasty dose of nervousness.

Toni muddled through a busy afternoon and few of

the albeit minor errors made could be attributed to Sandy's inexperience. It was a relief to escape but the symptoms of mild panic surfaced again in the super-market, causing Toni to throw all sorts of extraordi-nary items from the gourmet food department into her trolley and then gape momentarily in horror at the amount of money the checkout girl requested. Having paid for and transported her groceries home, Toni then began to worry about how her house looked.

Josh hadn't been to her home in four years and he'd only ever come to visit her mother. The house had changed considerably since then. Her mother's clutter was gone. The old-fashioned furnishings and decor had gone. What would Josh think of the adventurous colour scheme Toni had been inspired to try after eve-ning classes on interior decoration? The dark blue cabinets in the kitchen teamed with the canary yellow walls? The vivid Aztec design on the curtains in the adjoining living area with the terracotta-coloured so-fas and moss green walls?

Toni deposited the hastily chosen bags of gourmet supplies on the oversized butcher's block table in the kitchen and hurried to put a match to the kindling set in the open fireplace. She ignored Bessie's plaintive conversation. Heavens she'd completely forgotten to buy any wine! Josh was a wine buff. She'd be too embarrassed to even admit to bottles of highly dubi-ous quality wine lurking at the rear of her pantry. Why hadn't she ever taken an evening class on wine appreciation?

At least she'd done more than one season at the Culinary Classroom. Toni loved cooking and she was reasonably confident she could produce something of interest even to a gourmet of Josh's ilk. At least, if he helped to prepare it, she'd have an excuse if it did fail to pass muster.

Toni felt increasingly nervous. She'd never invited Josh to a meal before because she'd instinctively known that the offer would be turned down. It would have been turned down because Josh would instinctively have known that Toni had been offering more than a meal. Why had he accepted the invitation now? And why had Toni given it?

Because something had changed. A shift in the balance of their relationship. Because it seemed as if Josh needed something that possibly only Toni could provide. She didn't know what it was that he needed but she had to find out. And if there was any way she could provide it, she would.

'I've brought some wine.'

Toni looked at the bottle in amazement. 'Pink champagne! I've got some of that in my pantry. I didn't think it would rate a mention in your expert opinion on drinkability.'

'I like it,' Josh said firmly. 'It's what my parents always bought to celebrate anything really important. I was allowed to taste it when I was just a kid and it made me feel pretty special.' Josh dropped a fond gaze towards the bottle.

'It's fine with me.' Toni took the chilled bottle with a smile. 'I like it, too.'

Josh followed Toni into the kitchen. 'You've changed the house a bit.'

'Mmm. Too much, maybe. I got a bit carried away.'

'I love it.' Josh gazed around. 'It's bright and warm. It feels like a real home.'

'It is,' Toni answered simply. 'I've lived here for so long I can't imagine living anywhere else. It was always just Mum and me. She moved in here after my father died when I was three. The house is small but the garden's huge. I spend most of my time out there.' She held up the bottle. 'Shall I open this?'

'Let me.' Josh twisted off the foil cap. 'Look! A plastic cork!'

Toni laughed, 'I'd better find some plastic glasses.'

Josh looked at the scattering of items on the bench. 'Horseradish sauce and Camembert cheese. What are we going to cook?'

'Chicken and Camembert pastries with strawberry sauce,' Toni said confidently. 'I got the recipe at the cooking school I went to last year.'

Josh nodded. 'Nice.' He appeared to be concentrating hard on pouring the wine, his expression neutral.

'You don't fancy it, do you?' Toni asked anxiously. 'I should have got venison or a beef fillet or something.'

'God, no.' Josh handed Toni a wine glass brimming with bright pink liquid. She could hear the bubbles fizzing enthusiastically.

'Would you rather have something else?' Toni asked. 'Be honest, Josh. I've got heaps of stuff in the pantry and fridge.'

He gave her a long, steady look. 'I have no intention of being anything but honest tonight, Toni. You know what I'd really like? To go with this?' He raised his glass in a salute. 'Something real. Something with good memories attached to it. What I'd like,' Josh announced dramatically, 'is a big fry-up. Bacon and eggs.'

'And sausages?'

'And hash browns and French toast.'

'I've got lots of mushrooms,' Toni said grinning. 'We could put a tomato on one side and pretend it's healthy.'

'But we don't have to eat the tomato,' Josh decided. 'Not unless we really want to.'

'Sounds fantastic,' Toni smiled. 'I haven't had hash browns since I was a child.'

'Neither have I. Let's do it.'

'Let's,' Toni agreed. 'You start grating potatoes. I'll find the bacon and sausages.'

'We'll have to cook them in butter,' Josh stated. 'None of that healthy olive oil.'

'Perish the thought,' Toni agreed gaily. 'And if we can find any other way of piling on a few more grams of fat, let's do it. Life's too short to worry about cholesterol.'

'I knew you understood me better than anyone, Toni. That's why I love you. Where's the grater?'

But Toni didn't move. She simply stared at Josh.

'What's up?' Josh put down the potato he was holding. 'What did I say?'

'You said you loved me,' Toni said faintly.

'I'm being honest.' Josh suddenly looked far younger than he'd ever seemed to Toni. Young…and vulnerable. And inexplicably sad. 'I do love you. I always have, I think.'

Toni's chest felt tight. It was hard to breathe, let alone speak. 'I love you, too, Josh.'

'I know.' The sadness was still there. Toni couldn't understand it. She had to try and banish it. Tentatively, she stretched out her hand. She wanted to touch his face, to draw his head close enough to touch his lips with her own. Josh caught hold of her hand, pressed it against his cheek and turned his head so that his lips pressed against her palm. He closed his eyes and Toni held her breath as she waited for them to open. Waited to see if the shadow of pain had receded. It had. Josh even managed a crooked smile.

'I'm starving,' he told her. 'How do you make French Toast?'

'We…uh…we need some eggs. And milk,' Toni tried to concentrate. 'And the frying-pan.' Had Josh been simply talking about their friendship? Was this a signal that the bond between them might be deep but could never be anything greater than that?

'We'd better cook the bacon and sausages first, though, and put them in the oven to keep hot.'

'Right.' Josh gave her fingers a squeeze as he dropped her hand. 'I'll do that. Why don't you pour us another glass of lolly water?'

The meal was disgustingly delicious. They balanced their plates on their knees, sitting in front of the fire, pushing Bertie and Bessie out of the way at regular intervals as the cats tried to share the source of tempting aromas. Josh's shirtsleeves were rolled up. His tie and jacket had been discarded onto the back of one of the sofas. His shoes lay haphazardly nearby.

They ate crispy curls of bacon with their fingers, mopped up egg yolk with chunks of fried bread and ignored the tomatoes.

'That,' Josh declared finally, 'was heavenly.'

Toni smiled. 'The condemned man ate a hearty meal.' She watched as Josh put his plate aside and Bessie sniffed the tomato wedges, dismissing them

with a disdainful flick of her tail. The small cat fixed
Josh with a baleful glare but Josh was staring at Toni.

'What am I condemned to?' His tone was light but
the expression in his dark eyes was unreadable.

'The dishes.' Toni handed him her plate. He put it
on top of his own and Bessie pounced on the leftover
sausage, transporting it swiftly out of the room with
Bertie in hot pursuit.

'He knows what he wants.' Toni laughed. 'I don't
have the heart to stop him.' She leaned forward, picking up a log to throw on the fire.

'I know what I want, too.' The intensity of the
softly spoken words trickled up Toni's spine. She
turned, straightening her body, to find Josh kneeling,
his face close to her own. He raised his hand, touch-
ing Toni's cheek—an echo of her earlier gesture towards him. As he had done, Toni felt the compulsion
to turn her head so that her lips brushed his palm. To
close her eyes so that the sensation could be fully
appreciated.

Somehow, Josh's lips took the place of his palm
and the searching kiss was gladly answered by Toni.
She allowed herself the luxury of running her fingers
through the waves of soft, dark hair as she raised
herself to her knees to meet and follow the kiss, press-
ing closer as she felt Josh's hands grip her shoulders
more urgently.

Toni had never known that a man's touch could
bring such a sense of aching arousal. She'd known
for years how sensitive her skin was to Josh's prox-
imity—to his casual touch. She'd even been aware
that other feelings had stirred deeply, sometimes painfully, and if they couldn't be suppressed they could
leave a burning frustration. But this...

Toni's breath caught as Josh's lips moved to her neck. Slow, gentle kisses that lingered on the thundering pulse in her throat. His hands stroked the length of her spine and she felt the strength of his grip on her bottom as he pulled her against him. She could feel the power, the heat of his arousal and she groaned at the barrier their clothes still provided.

Josh's hand stilled instantly. 'Toni?' His voice was raw. 'Do you want me to stop?' His laugh was grating. 'If you do, then tell me now because otherwise—'

Toni pressed her fingers against his lips to silence him. 'I don't want you to stop,' she whispered shakily. 'Please…don't stop.'

Her fingers moved to the buttons on his shirt and his gaze held hers solemnly as his hands mirrored her action on the buttons of her silk blouse. The task was completed slowly, reverently, and Josh turned, flicking off the lamp that had illuminated the joyous discovery of each other's bodies. Now they were bathed only in the flickering glow of the firelight.

Josh moved away abruptly. He was searching the pocket of his suit jacket. Toni shivered, feeling abandoned, but then understood. Protection. Something she wouldn't have even thought of. Of course, Josh would have the necessary supplies. With his social life he'd have been a fool not to be prepared at all times. Toni knew she should feel somehow belittled, insulted that he might have expected this development, but she didn't care. Nothing mattered any more except that she and Josh were together.

A new urgency was spawned with their renewed touch and Toni arched against Josh with a joyous cry, hearing only dimly the almost desperate whisper of her name. She'd thought there could be no pleasure as exquisite as this, the feeling of being home—at last. Of arriving at the only place she'd ever wanted to be.

But she was wrong. As Josh's hands clutched her and his body shuddered in release she felt herself spiralling into a bliss she had never dreamt existed. He was kissing her again now. Deeply. Tenderly. Holding her face and murmuring softly.

'Thank you,' he repeated yet again, with a long, contented sigh. 'I knew perfection existed somewhere but I could never have experienced it without you.'

Toni was still aware of the rapid beating of his heart against her skin, of the slick warmth where their bodies still joined. She wanted to cry out as he withdrew slowly. She was losing something much greater than the intimate contact but she couldn't understand what it was.

This was the beginning, surely, of something wonderful. Why did she have such a deep foreboding that it was also an end?

'I love you, Josh,' she said, a little desperately, trying to cling to what they had just shared.

'I know.' His tone was gentle. 'I love you, too. And thanks to you I can honestly say I know what that really means now. Thank you.'

'Stop saying that,' Toni pleaded. 'You make it sound like it was all one-sided. That I've given you something that wasn't returned.'

'Perhaps you've given me more than you realise,' Josh told her quietly. 'A moment of perfection. One in which the past doesn't matter and future doesn't exist. The knowledge of what real love is all about. What a relationship could be. It's a gift I never thought I'd have and I want you to know how much it means to me. And I hope…I hope you'll forgive me one day.'

Toni stared at him, her fear surfacing. 'There's nothing to forgive. I don't care about the past. It's the future that matters. It's never too late to start again, Josh.'

'No, it's not.' He was staring at her with a peculiar intensity. 'Never forget that, my love. No matter what.'

CHAPTER SEVEN

IT WAS never too late to start again.

And the start had been more than Toni had ever dreamed of. She and Josh had found each other. After all these years they were together. Toni might not have the wealth of experience in relationships that Josh had gathered but she knew beyond any shadow of doubt that this was as good as it could possibly get.

This was what Oliver and Sophie had found together. Possibly even better. Toni couldn't believe that any couple could have found the depth of love she and Josh shared. This was the stuff of marriage. Lifetime commitment. Till death us do part.

Toni had never felt happier. Or more nervous. How would Josh act when he got to work this morning? How should she respond? Was their new intimacy going to be instantly obvious to their colleagues? Josh hadn't mentioned marriage. His aversion to the state of matrimony was something of a joke. It might be embarrassing for him to back down and maybe he didn't want to. Toni could live with that. Much as she'd held fantasies of floating down a church aisle, with Josh waiting for her at the end, it was just a ceremony after all. What really mattered was what came later. The lifetime bond. They could have that without marriage. They *did* have it.

Toni dressed with all the agony of indecision a teenager might have displayed before a first date. She ruffled the contents of her wardrobe with increasing frustration. This was a new start and she wanted something appropriate to wear. Most of the items she scrutinised looked as if they needed to be donated to a rag collection and others were just too boring. The weather precluded any contemplation of a summer dress.

Billowing white clouds with ominous black edges were doing their best to cover patches of brilliantly blue sky. And it was freezing. Toni finally settled on a flared black skirt, a white blouse and her favourite winter jersey—a soft mohair creation in bright scarlet. She zipped up knee-high black boots, the heels of which gave her height an extra three inches. Toni left her hair loose, enjoying the way the shining black tresses waved softly onto her shoulders, and she took the extra time necessary to apply a touch more make-up than usual.

Was it excitement that gave her eyes that new sparkle and depth? Or was it just that it was still a novelty to see the shade of hazel they were when not filtered through thick spectacle lenses. Josh was right. They did have flickers of gold in them—just like whisky in sunlight. For the first time in her life, Toni Marsh felt truly beautiful. Desirable. She couldn't wait to get to work.

The temperature had dropped even further by the time Toni arrived at the medical centre. She went through all the rooms, turning on the fan heaters. Outboard was calling loudly from the staffroom where he was shut in at night so he didn't trip the alarm system.

The kitten was already living up to his name as Toni picked him up for a quick cuddle. He sank his front paws into the soft, red jersey and kneaded it ecstatically. Toni tucked the plaster cast on his back leg into the crook of her arm. Outboard was an astonishingly sociable little cat. The more company he got, the happier he was. Toni felt guilty that he was left alone at night but the amount of company during the day probably more than made up for it. He was a perfect waiting-room cat, ready to respond to a friendly overture from anyone.

The rasp of the small tongue on her hand prompted Toni to rub her chin on the silky black head. Outboard produced a curious gargling noise as he tried to purr more loudly.

The quick rattle of sleet against the window made Toni glance up in time to see Sophie and Oliver arrive. She could see Sophie grimacing at the weather as she climbed out of the car. September was a funny month. After the tantalising promise of spring in August, they could often be plunged dramatically back into the depths of winter with vicious frosts, hail storms or torrential rain. Sophie was rubbing at her arms and stamping her feet while she waited for Oliver to lock the car. Their breath was visible in bursts of white steam as they tipped their heads close enough to touch and both laughed at some shared joke.

Toni would normally have felt a poignant exclusion at the evidence of their closeness. Not today. She planted a kiss on Outboard's head as she filled the jug with one hand and flicked the switch to boil the water. She knew what it was like now. She wasn't on the outside, envying the bond others shared. She had her own and it was better than anyone else's could possibly be.

'You're an angel, Toni.' Oliver gave her a resounding kiss on the cheek. 'All the heaters on and coffee ready. If I weren't married already you wouldn't stand a chance.'

Sophie looked on, grinning. 'I love your jersey, Toni. What a perfect colour for a day like this. Isn't it *cold*?'

'Miserable,' Toni agreed happily. She'd never felt less miserable in her life. Making coffee for Sophie and Oliver, she'd missed seeing Josh drive into the car park. When he came into the staffroom she gasped in delight. So did Sophie.

'Josh!' Sophie cried. 'Where did you find *those*?'

He held an armful of spring flowers—an enormous bouquet of daffodils, jonquils and cheers. The scent mingled with the aroma of coffee and quickly overpowered it.

'They had buckets of them outside a dairy when I drove past,' Josh told them. 'I bought every bunch.' His gaze caught Toni's and held it. 'The weather's so awful I thought we could do with a reminder that it is still officially springtime.'

Sophie had her nose buried in the glow of golden and white blooms. 'Glorious,' she breathed. 'Makes you think of lambs gambolling and ducklings and foals.'

Oliver groaned. 'There you go again. Babies on the brain.'

Josh was smiling. 'It's a good time to think of babies.'

Toni's breath caught in a painful jerk. Was *Josh* thinking of babies? He'd been so careful about protecting her last night but had something changed about how he saw his future? *Their* future?

'A new season,' she affirmed quietly, smiling directly at Josh. 'A new beginning.'

'Let's put them out on your counter, Toni,' Josh suggested. 'That way we can all enjoy them.'

Toni nodded happily. She put down the kitten who made a beeline for Sophie's lap. Everybody could enjoy the flowers but they would be on *her* counter. Her hands brushed his as Josh transferred the bundle. The contact from his brown eyes added a further caress.

'You look stunning in red,' he told her.

'Thanks.' Toni's glanced darted towards Oliver and Sophie. Surely they were as aware as she was of the current between herself and Josh? But the Spencers had eyes only for each other. The mention of babies seemed to have propelled them into a silent communication that precluded any interest in what was happening around them.

Janet arrived as Toni positioned the huge jug of flowers in full view of the reception area.

'Och, aren't they bonny?' Janet pulled off her mittens but left the knitted woollen hat on her head. 'It's the last thing I expected to see today. I'm sure it's going to snow.'

'In September? I doubt it.' Toni shook her head.

'Stranger things have happened.' Josh came into the office and nodded approvingly at the floral display. 'Nice,' he murmured.

'It *feels* like it's going to snow.' Janet pulled off her hat and tried to smooth her wild curls into submission. 'I should know. I've had years of Scottish winters to hone my skills of prediction. I hope it does. The boys would be thrilled.'

'That reminds me!' Josh snapped his fingers.

'Aren't you planning to get the boys a computer for their birthday, Jan?'

Janet's smile was wistful. 'I'm saving up. Their birthday's only two months away, though. Maybe I'll go for a PlayStation instead. Computers cost the earth.'

'Maybe not,' Josh said casually. 'I'm thinking of trading mine in. I thought the boys might like it.'

'What's wrong with it?' Toni asked in surprise. 'It's not even a year old.'

Josh seemed absorbed in reading the appointment book. 'There's a new Pentium out that's rather exciting. A year in computers makes them virtually obsolete. It would still be great for the twins, though,' he assured Janet.

'I couldn't afford it,' Janet said doubtfully.

'I'd like to give it to them,' Josh offered. 'If it's OK with you.'

Toni could see the conflicting reactions in Janet's expression. She knew how much of a financial struggle Janet found single motherhood. She also knew how fiercely independent their practice nurse was.

'No. I couldn't accept that, Josh,' Janet said carefully. 'You do too much for us as it is. Maybe I could buy it off you.'

'OK.' Josh nodded as though the details were unimportant. 'As long as it gets to them some time. Technology's the way education is going these days. Adam and Rory are bright kids. They deserve the chance to get ahead.'

Janet was smiling. 'Thanks, Josh. That means a lot. I know they're bright. I can't understand why they're having so much trouble at school. The staff are talk-

ing about putting them into a remedial reading pro-
gramme.'

'They'll come right,' Josh assured her.

Toni switched the phones through and one immediately began to ring. Josh listened to her field the
call and tapped her on the shoulder.

'I'll see Mr Collins,' he told her. 'Make him my
first patient for the day.'

Janet's mouth was gaping as she watched Josh
leave. 'Did I hear correctly? Josh *volunteering* to see
Mr Collins?'

'Stranger things have happened.' Toni grinned. 'I
think Dr Cooper might be turning over a new leaf.
Celebrating spring. He was the one responsible for
those flowers.'

'Hmm.' Janet's face crumpled thoughtfully. 'Must
be a new woman, then.'

'Must be,' Toni agreed. 'Let's hope Mr Collins ap-
preciates the spin-off.'

Mr Collins arrived on the dot of 9.15, looking very
pleased with his early appointment. He emerged from
Josh's office twenty minutes later looking ready to
burst with pride.

'You'll have to make me some appointments at the
hospital, lassie,' he told Toni loudly. He looked
around to make sure everyone in the waiting room
was paying attention. 'I'm going to need a twelve-
lead ECG, a Holter monitor, an exercise test, an echo-
cardiogram and—' Mr Collins stood on tiptoe with
excitement '…possibly even a *nuclear scan*!'

'My word.' Toni's expression was suitably impressed. 'That all sounds a bit serious.'

Mr Collins nodded importantly. 'Dr Cooper and I
feel that the investigations are justified.' He tapped

the telephone in front of Toni. 'Have you got a direct line through to the cardiology department there, girl?'

Toni suppressed her giggle. 'Let me see what I can do, Mr Collins.'

The temperature seemed to drop even lower as the morning progressed. A blast of cold air reminded Toni of the conditions outside every time the front door opened. The atmosphere inside was anything but frigid. Everyone exclaimed over the flowers, appreciated the heating Toni still had running on full power, enjoyed the attentions of Outboard and forgot to complain about having to wait, even though the appointment times began to run up to thirty minutes late. Toni smiled at one young mother who sat breast-feeding a baby. She was being avidly observed by an obviously pregnant woman on the other side of the room who was dressed in a rather startling orange and gold caftan.

'My baby's due in November,' the observer told the young mother. 'The eighteenth. It'll be a Scorpio. That's a water sign, you know. What sun sign has your baby got?'

'I've no idea.' The baby's mother looked somewhat dazed.

Toni turned away to hide her smile. Pagan Ellis had been a patient of Sophie's since early in her pregnancy and Toni enjoyed the times she enlivened the waiting area. If she wasn't meditating in the corner she had the ability to draw everyone into a common conversation.

'When was he born?' Pagan demanded.

'May sixteenth.'

'Ah, a Taurus.' Pagan nodded. 'Yes, he looks like a Taurus.'

'Really?' The baby's mother sounded surprised, as well she might. The baby was feeding vigorously and only the back of his downy head was visible.

'He likes his food,' Pagan explained. 'He'll probably grow up to be a real gourmet.'

Just like Josh, Toni mused. He was a Taurus as well. Perhaps there *was* something in this astrology business. Then again, Josh hadn't wanted anything fancy last night. Toni could feel a flush of warmth, although she was standing well away from the office heater.

'Oliver hasn't signed this prescription form.' Sandy Smith was looking anxious again. 'I'm supposed to fax it through to a pharmacy. What shall I do?'

'Take it in to him,' Toni advised. 'Knock on his door first, though, in case he's examining a patient.' Keying information into the computer from another patient, Toni was keeping half an ear on the lively conversation in the waiting room.

'He might be a musician or artist. He'll be an expert on beautiful things and probably make a lot of money out of investments.' Pagan was suddenly distracted by the arrival of Outboard. 'Oh, aren't *you* beautiful?' she exclaimed.

Toni clicked her mouse on the save option. Josh had never made a lot of money out of investments. Or if he had he'd given it away. Free consultations or prepaid private referrals for patients. He didn't own a house. His car was definitely the worse for wear at present and he was even trying to give away his relatively new and very expensive computer system. Toni shook her head. He *was* an expert on beautiful things, however. Especially women. And *she* was one of them.

The new arrival at St David's was greeted with a brilliant smile. 'How are you, Mrs Bradshaw?'

The very elderly woman sniffed and looked dubiously at Toni. 'If I was well enough I wouldn't be here, would I?'

'No, I suppose not.' Toni's smile dimmed a fraction. 'Would you like to take a seat, Mrs Bradshaw? Dr Spencer shouldn't be too long.'

Mrs Bradshaw gave the spring blooms an offended stare and took a seat beside Pagan Ellis. Outboard went straight for the thickly stockinged leg, only to be nudged aside.

'Animals shouldn't be in a doctor's surgery,' the old woman muttered loudly. 'It's unhygienic.'

Pagan was looking amused. She turned her attention away from the gourmet baby to her new neighbour. Toni hid a fresh smile. She doubted very much that the cheerless Mrs Bradshaw would have any idea about her sun sign but Pagan Ellis would probably be the one who could find out.

Josh came through the archway to collect his next patient. 'Wendy, would you like to bring Matthew through now?'

The young mother gazed down at her breast. 'Wouldn't you know it? After keeping me awake all night, he's finally gone to sleep.' She eased the infant free and fumbled for her bra fastening.

'Let me hold Matthew for you,' Josh offered.

Toni stared as Josh tucked the sleeping bundle into the crook of his arm and made soothing, nonsensical noises.

Pagan Ellis was also staring. 'Wow! That does amazing things to your aura, Josh.'

Toni swallowed the lump in her throat. Maybe

Pagan wasn't so loopy after all. Even from across the room Toni could sense the change in atmosphere as Josh held the baby, could sense the softening of his expression even though she couldn't see his face. Toni didn't dare try to catch his eye as he escorted Wendy past the counter. The desire she felt to hold a baby—Josh's baby—was so powerful it scared her. It would probably scare Josh even more if he caught the gist of her thoughts.

Lunch was a rushed affair. Having caught up with the morning's list, the doctors only had fifteen minutes together in the staffroom. Janet had already gone to organise her afternoon.

'It took me half an hour to make all those appointments for Mr Collins,' Toni grumbled with mock complaint to Josh. 'Does he really need them?'

'No.' Josh was unrepentant. 'But it'll keep him happy for weeks. He'll probably be dining out on the accounts of his investigations for years.' Josh sat back in his chair. 'It'll also give us great baseline measurements if he does actually come up with a genuine problem in the future.'

'The panel-beaters rang.' Toni unwrapped the Camembert cheese and crackers she'd brought for her lunch. The cheese reminded her of the ingredients for the dinner she'd planned to cook for Josh last night. The dinner which had been hijacked into something quite different. 'Your car's fixed,' she continued hurriedly, feeling colour creeping into her cheeks. 'You can pick it up any time.'

'I'm not in any hurry,' Josh said calmly. 'I quite like my loan vehicle.'

Oliver guffawed. 'What? That heap of junk? What is it, a 1960 Ford Escort van?'

'Something like that. It used to be the firm's vehicle. At least I think that's what that leftover lettering says. You can't see too well through the rust.'

'You can hear the gears changing two blocks away.' Oliver chuckled. 'And I'll bet the speedo stops at fifty kilometres per hour. Hardly your usual style, Josh.'

'I like it,' Josh affirmed. 'It has character.'

'Gosh, I'm starving.' Sophie licked her fingers as she swallowed the last of her filled roll. 'Can I have your piece of carrot cake, Oliver?'

'No.' Oliver snatched his plate away from Sophie's hand. 'It's mine. You had yours for morning tea.'

'Uh—oh. Honeymoon's over,' Josh said with a grin.

Sophie glared at Oliver. 'But I'm *hungry*.'

'Would you like my sandwich, Sophie?'

'Ooh, thanks.' Sophie hesitated. 'Aren't you going to eat anything, Josh?'

'I'm not hungry.' Josh threw Toni a quick glance. 'I had a rather special dinner last night. I don't want to spoil the memory by eating something as dull as a sandwich.'

Toni felt her blush returning. She fiddled with her coffee mug. 'Shall I tell the panel-beater to send someone over to swap the cars?'

'That would be great. I'll just have to get something out of the back.' Josh pushed his plate towards Sophie with a grin, before looking back at Toni. 'I couldn't get to sleep last night after I got home so I had a bit of a tidy-up in my wardrobe. I've got a bag of clothes I don't need. Do you know where to go if you want to donate them to charity?'

'I'll call the mission,' Toni offered. 'They might

collect them. It's funny, I was thinking of doing the same thing myself this morning.' She didn't add that she'd also had great difficulty in getting to sleep last night after Josh had finally gone home.

'Must be spring,' Sophie observed, her mouth full of sandwich.

'I'll get the bag now,' Josh decided. He stood up and suddenly staggered sideways. He would have fallen but for Oliver's arm shooting out to steady him.

'Hell, what was in that coffee?' Oliver was on his feet now. 'Are you all right, mate?'

'Sure.' Josh's hand was gripping the side of the table. His face had paled. 'I didn't notice my foot had gone to sleep, that's all.' He looked down and waggled his right foot, his face twisted in a pained grimace. 'Now I've got pins and needles.' He stamped his foot and appeared to balance himself carefully before he let go of the table. 'I've obviously been sitting here for far too long. I'll get back to work.'

Oliver nodded, apparently unconcerned. Sophie was looking at the remaining cheese and crackers on Toni's plate. Only Toni was staring at Josh, anxiety clouding her eyes. Had nobody else noticed the sheen of perspiration which Josh now casually brushed off his forehead? Was she the only one who'd seen that flash of fear in his face when Oliver had gripped his arm to steady him? The moment had passed and Josh now looked as unconcerned as his medical colleagues, but Toni found it less easy to dismiss.

The vague feeling of disturbance stayed with her throughout the afternoon despite Josh's apparent cheerfulness. She watched closely when he ducked out and came back carrying a lumpy plastic rubbish sack, tied at the top.

'The old clothes,' he explained. 'I'll just stick them in the corner for the moment.'

'OK.' Toni was still watching. The waiting room had emptied for the day and the phones were quiet. Outboard had positioned himself beside the heater and was watching hopefully for a late arrival. Josh looked at him as he passed.

'He's a neat little guy, isn't he?' Josh put the large bag down in Toni's office. 'I couldn't believe it when I saw him sitting on Mrs Bradshaw's knee this morning.'

'Neither could Mrs Bradshaw.' Toni laughed. 'I'm not sure but I *think* she almost smiled.'

Josh laughed and Toni relaxed. He appeared quite steady on his feet now. In fact, he looked better than he had in quite some time. Almost content. Perhaps there was nothing to worry about.

'You know, I can't believe I ever called you Swampy,' Josh told her softly. 'You are the complete opposite of anything remotely damp or dark. You brighten things up even without that jersey on.' He checked they were still alone and then lowered his voice suggestively. '*Especially* without the jersey on.'

Toni laughed with delight. Of course there was nothing to worry about. The look in Josh's eyes told her that he'd forgotten nothing of their time together. His words confirmed it.

'You're a very special woman, Antoinette. I hope—'

Toni didn't find out what Josh was hoping. Janet came in, brandishing a small pad of paper.

'What on earth is the narcotic prescription pad doing in the treatment room? It should be in the safe.' She crouched down and pulled the square of carpet free to expose the floor safe. 'Damn, I've forgotten the combination. I really don't have time for this.'

Josh moved as though to help and then stopped, putting his hand out suddenly to touch the wall. Toni's eyes widened in alarm. Had he lost his balance again? She was still close enough to speak quietly without Janet overhearing.

'What's wrong, Josh?' she asked urgently.

'Nothing,' Josh muttered fiercely. His gaze almost burned Toni. She could not fail to receive the warning not to pursue the matter. Josh turned his gaze to the files on the shelf, still balancing himself with one hand on the wall.

'Eleven, seventy-three, right,' he told Janet off-handedly. 'Then four, twenty-six, left.' He hooked a file out and tucked it under his arm.

'Thanks.' Janet lifted the lid of the safe. She peered in, before depositing the pad. 'It's a bit of a mess in here,' she announced. 'We'd have trouble finding something if we needed it in a hurry.'

'I'll tidy it up,' Toni said distractedly. She was still watching Josh. He was lying—she was sure of it—but she knew how Josh would react if she pushed him, and the last thing Toni wanted right now was an argument with Josh.

'Do it tomorrow,' Josh advised. 'It's getting late and it's time we all went home. Look, I think you were right, Janet. It *is* starting to snow.'

Sure enough, the unusual climatic event was in progress. Fluffy, large flakes of snow were drifting past the window.

'Fantastic!' Janet crowed excitedly. 'I must go and get the boys. Oh, I hope it settles.'

Sophie came out with her last patient. 'Have you

seen the snow?' she asked happily. 'We'd better all
get home before the roads get too slippery.'

'Good idea.' Josh nodded. 'Off you go. I'll see you
all tomorrow.'

His gaze rested on Toni. She could feel herself
warmed by the tenderness she saw as he waited until
Sophie left the office. Her pulse tripped as she held
her breath. Was he going to suggest they get together
again this evening? But his gaze now held an apology.

'I'm afraid I've got a few things to get sorted tonight. I'm going to use the time before my meeting
to catch up on some paperwork.' Josh winked at Toni.
'I might even have time to sort out the chaos in my
desk drawers so that they match the rest of my office.
Have we got any spare boxes?'

'There are some in the storeroom.' Toni hesitated,
rapidly considering whether she could offer to help.
Would Josh be annoyed if she made it so obvious that
she wanted his company? Maybe he'd think she
wanted to keep an eye on him, looking for another
opportunity to quiz him about his health. Toni's disappointment increased painfully as her instincts told
her not to offer her assistance this time. She attempted
to hide her reaction but she knew she had failed when
the apology in Josh's expression intensified.

Toni tried to smile. 'It doesn't matter that you're
busy tonight, Josh. There's always tomorrow.'

Josh just smiled. 'Hey, Toni?'

'Mmm?'

'Wear that red jersey again. Please? For me?'

'Sure.' Toni would do anything Josh asked of her.
Any time.

_'Tomorrow?' Josh added quietly.

Toni nodded as seriously as Josh's tone had invited.

'Tomorrow,' she confirmed.

CHAPTER EIGHT

TOMORROW never comes.

The thought struck Toni with a chilling finality as she drove home carefully. The headlights on her car illuminated a scene straight from a Christmas card or the inside of one of those little glass balls that you shook to make it snow. The fat, feathery flakes were settling fast on the icy surface of the road. Toni was glad she didn't have far to drive. The slope of one of the only hill suburbs in Christchurch would soon be impassable.

Bertie and Bessie were unimpressed by the dramatic change in the weather, but Toni was too distracted to pay much attention to their vociferous protests. The house was freezing and Toni made up the fire, before doing anything else. She scrunched up sheets of newspaper and then laid kindling over the paper. She didn't really want to light the fire, however. She would never be able to sit in the flickering light and warmth of an open fire again without missing Josh.

She missed him now, with a deep ache she couldn't ignore.

'Oh, for goodness' sake,' she muttered irritably, scooping Bessie from the wood basket. 'He had something to do tonight. It's just one night. There's always tomorrow. And tomorrow and tomorrow.' Toni sat back on her heels and stared at the unlit fire.

But tomorrow never came. Her feeling of loss

stemmed from much more than the knowledge she was missing an evening of Josh's company. They'd only just declared their love. They had a whole lifetime to share it. So what *was* disturbing Toni so deeply? The fact that Josh might be unwell? But his cold symptoms had gone completely. He looked better than he had for weeks. He seemed happier than he had for weeks. Almost…serene.

It was an odd word to think of applying to Josh Cooper. Ebullient, gregarious, funny, generous, sometimes moody. Always loyal and honest, compassionate and clever. All of those words applied frequently. But…serene? Toni knew Josh better than that. Something had changed. Dramatically. And she knew instinctively that she had precipitated the change. But serenity wasn't an emotion prompted by the recognition and declaration of a long-held passion. It didn't fit with the beginning of anything. It was more appropriate to an ending, an ending that was understood and accepted.

Toni stood up to dissuade Bertie from trying to climb up her back. Her pacing took her into the kitchen where the two sleek cats positioned themselves hopefully in front of the fridge. Absentmindedly, Toni turned to the pantry and took out the bag of dried cat food. She poured some into the bowl on the floor but neither cat moved a muscle.

'OK.' Toni snatched a tin out of the pantry. 'But this is it, you guys. If you don't eat real cat food tonight you can both go hungry.'

Like Josh had done at lunchtime. Again. Last night had been the first time Toni had seen him eat in ages. But then he had wolfed down their outrageous dinner with evident enjoyment. What had she said? 'The condemned man ate a hearty meal.' Toni sighed. Something wasn't right.

There were little things that should add up to something. Like those flowers which had wilted sadly during a day in an overheated waiting room. Like the special attention Josh had shown his patients—even the impossible Mr Collins. Like the offer to give his computer to Janet's children.

Toni turned the worry around in her mind as she took out the chicken breasts which had been unused last night. Bertie and Bessie approved the action. They snaked around her ankles, trying to outdo each other with their demonstrations of devotion. Toni eyed the chicken. She eyed the cats. Then she looked at their full, untouched food bowls.

'Oh, what the hell,' she told them. 'I'm not hungry and chicken doesn't keep.' She diced the boneless breasts and dumped the pile of meat onto a fresh plate. The cats didn't bother looking up as she walked away. The purrs that emerged would have done Outboard credit. Toni had, at last, done the right thing.

Toni changed her clothes. She kept on her warm red jersey but swapped the skirt for jeans. She discarded the high-heeled boots and laced up her trainers, putting on a thick anorak before searching out a woollen hat and gloves. She needed to *do* something. A walk in the snow would be fun and was an unusual enough activity to distract her. It was an odd experience, crunching through the snow on the road. She was by no means alone. The streetlamps were providing plenty of light now that the snow had stopped falling so thickly. The neighbourhood children were out in force, enjoying the novelty. A snowman was taking shape in a nearby reserve. Janice Reynolds was standing by her front gate, watching all the activity.

'How are you, Janice?' Toni queried gently after the two women had greeted each other.

'I'm coping,' Janice told her. 'Look at this.' Janice bent down and clicked her fingers. 'Come here, Max!'

A fat, black and white puppy waddled out from beneath a shrub. It shook itself to clear the layer of snow from its back, overbalanced and flopped onto its side, before wriggling joyously upright to launch itself towards the women. Toni chuckled and Janice smiled.

'A friend gave him to me yesterday. He said Max was just what I needed right now and I think he was right. Having to look after something other than yourself makes it impossible to feel too lonely.'

Toni nodded. Hadn't she always looked after Josh? As much as he'd allowed her to, anyway. She stooped to pat the puppy.

'Ben would have loved you,' she told Max. 'He always wanted a dog.'

'He did, didn't he?' Janice sighed. 'We never got one, though. There just seemed to be too much else to cope with.' She glanced at Toni cautiously. 'You know, I've been wondering whether Ben's crash really *was* an accident.'

'Have you?' Toni waited in some trepidation for Janice's response.

'Silly, isn't it?' Janice said with an embarrassed smile. 'It's amazing, all the things I've been thinking. Like what if those test results had been wrong. That virus he had gave him symptoms just like Jim had in the beginning now that I think about it.'

Toni made a sympathetic sound.

'It doesn't need to mean anything, of course. Anyone can be clumsy and do things like knock over glasses.'

Toni agreed. Josh had done it. More than once.

'And lots of things can put you off your food and make it seem hard to swallow.'

Toni agreed again. When had Josh ever bothered to eat lunch at work? And she'd surprised *him* into almost choking on one occasion.

'And a virus could well give you shaky hands and affect your balance for a while.'

'Mmm.' All Toni could think of was Josh stumbling as he'd risen from the table earlier that day and the way he'd caught himself with his hand on the wall in her office that evening. She tried to clear the disturbing images. 'Would you *want* to know, Janice?' she asked softly. 'If it had been something else?'

Janice was silent for a moment. 'No,' she said finally. 'It's over now. I've got my life to get on with.' She smiled down at the puppy who was enthusiastically tugging on the gaping top of her gumboot. 'And I've got Max to look after. I'd better take him inside before he gets too cold.'

Toni carried on walking. Nobody had called their children in to get ready for bed yet.

The slope of the roadway was being used for sliding. Plastic rubbish bags and cardboard boxes were more numerous than genuine toboggans or snowboards.

Toni smiled at the activities but the excitement of the snow had gone for her. She had too much else on her mind. If anything, the twenty minutes of fresh air had sharpened her worries. She thought about Janice and Ben. She thought about Josh. She wondered whether he'd finished the work he'd planned to do that evening and whether he'd been caught by the snow and had had to walk home. Toni found she'd been walking in the direction of St David's. Her thoughts finally seemed to be coalescing but she was unsure of their direction as she continued to think about Josh. And Ben. And the rapport the two men had had.

There was a light on at St David's. More than one, in fact. If Josh had forgotten to turn them out, he would probably have also forgotten to activate the alarm system. Toni opened the front door with a tolerant shake of her head. Just as well she was there to put things right.

Toni nearly tripped over the large, black plastic bag Josh must have shifted from the office. She'd better remember to call the mission tomorrow. The bag was surprisingly heavy. He'd obviously had a good clean-out of his wardrobe. As Toni pulled it aside, the strip of plastic tying the top slipped loose and the bag gaped open. She peered in, frowning, and then lifted out the item of clothing on top of the neatly folded pile. A suit jacket. A dark grey, formal suit jacket, the one Josh had worn as best man only weeks ago. The one she'd taken to the dry-cleaners herself. The ticket was still pinned to the jacket's lapel.

Surely Josh had made a mistake. He couldn't intend this suit to go to charity. Toni smoothed out the jacket and lifted the matching trousers from the bag as well. She would hang them in Josh's office and make sure she checked with him in the morning. Toni knew the cleaners weren't due until tomorrow night but there was no point in taking the chance of having the bag disposed of accidentally.

Toni was startled to find Josh still in his office. She was shocked by the array of boxes surrounding his desk. They clearly contained everything that had been on the shelves of Josh's office. The shelves were completely bare.

'What on earth are you doing?' Toni exclaimed.

'Why are *you* here?' Josh demanded. 'Go away, Toni. I'm busy.'

'You look like you're moving out,' Toni said accusingly.

'Do I?' Josh was holding one of the drawers from his desk. He tipped it, letting the contents fall into the box he had ready. A shower of ballpoint pens, paper clips and a stapler landed with a clatter.

'What's going on, Josh?' Toni stepped further into the room and shut the door behind her. '*Are* you planning to leave?'

'I can't stay,' Josh said impatiently. 'Not now.'

'Why?' Toni tried to swallow her fear. 'Because of me?'

'Because of...' Josh yanked another drawer free of its runners. 'Because of lots of things.'

'Does this have something to do with Ben Reynolds?' Suddenly Toni understood the direction into which her thoughts had been trying to lead her. She could put a name to the fear she had suppressed.

'Drop it, Toni,' Josh growled. 'I'm doing this for you.'

'*What?*' Toni spat the word out in disbelief.

'Just go away,' Josh said wearily.

A wave of heat galvanised Toni. 'Don't tell me to go away, Josh Cooper,' she said furiously. 'You're planning to walk out on me without so much as an explanation. Well, I won't let you.' Toni stalked over to a chair, removed the box it was supporting with an angry gesture and sat down. She glared at Josh.

Josh put down the drawer he was holding. He turned his gaze away from Toni.

'I was going to write you a letter.' Josh nudged a pad of writing paper on the corner of his desk. A small white card dislodged itself and fluttered to the floor.

'I don't want a bloody letter,' Toni snapped. She stared at the card which had landed near her feet. It was a photograph, the photograph of herself and Josh taken at Oliver's and Sophie's wedding. Toni fought off a black wave of despair. '*Talk* to me, Josh,' she commanded. '*Now!*'

Josh sat down, very slowly, on the chair beside his desk. There was a distance of only a few feet between them but the gulf it represented was appallingly deep.

'All right,' Josh said bitterly. 'You're right, Toni. This *is* about you. About us. About Ben Reynolds.'

'I thought so,' Toni muttered. 'I knew there was a connection somewhere.' She was still staring at Josh. 'What did your father die of, Josh?'

'A heart attack.'

Toni frowned. It wasn't the answer she'd expected. Had she been wrong?

'A broken heart is probably more accurate,' Josh added calmly. 'He had no risk factors at all. I think he just wanted to escape.'

'Escape from what?'

Josh gave her a long, long look that chilled Toni to the bone. 'From watching my mother die.' Josh's tone was impassive. Clinical.

'And your mother died from?' Toni's voice was equally controlled. She knew the answer. She didn't want to hear it from Josh. But she knew she had no choice.

'From Huntington's chorea.'

The silence went on. And on. It was Josh who finally fractured it.

'My father escaped,' he said grimly. 'I was the only one left to watch my mother die. To see her trapped in a progressively more rigid body. She couldn't walk or speak. The liquid diet she was on couldn't prevent the gradual wasting away of her body. But she was still aware. She still knew me when I visited. Maybe she knew that I'd graduated from medical school. Maybe she was even proud of me.' Josh paused and swallowed with painful effort. 'That's something I'll never know. She died not long after that and it was then that I planned my own life.'

Josh straightened a little on his chair and seemed to collect himself.

'I knew there was no way on earth I'd ever put anyone through what my mother inflicted on myself and my father, however unintentional on her part. I wasn't going to let anyone—or anything—become dependent on me. I've never even kept a cat, for God's sake. I wasn't going to leave anyone to grieve. No loose ends.'

Josh snorted without amusement. 'I picked general practice so I would have enough money and plenty of time to indulge in whatever hobbies or recreational activities took my fancy. I bought the best cars I could afford and I partied with the best of them. I picked women who held no threat of upsetting the emotional equilibrium I'd created for myself. If they started wanting more I simply called it off.'

'The "M" word.' Toni almost smiled. So Josh's aversion to the state of matrimony hadn't been as irrational as it had seemed.

'It was only you that got under my guard, Toni,' Josh said sadly. 'You sneaked in with the way you cared about little things. Like that pot plant in my room here that you kept nurtured for years even when my mess practically buried it. Like the cup of coffee you always made for me first thing in the morning and the painkillers you'd offer so discreetly when you knew I had a hangover.' Josh was smiling at Toni now.

'It was that noticeboard of yours with all the photos. The joy you could take in other people's happiness or the births of their babies. The way you could get on with naughty young children or irritable old pensioners.' Josh leaned forward, his hands on his knees. 'It was the way you always gave far more than you took—from anyone. And it was the way you cared for your mother. I knew what you were going through and I admired you so much for that. It was more than I'd been able to do for my own mother.'

'I couldn't have done it without you,' Toni said softly. 'And you gave me my job back. Gave me a life to go back to after she died.'

'I needed to have you around,' Josh admitted. 'I missed you so much that year. I couldn't let you get too close but I couldn't do without you either.'

'I never asked for more than you were prepared to give me.' Toni felt the need to defend herself. 'Did I?'

Josh didn't seem to hear her question. 'You thought

that Ben might have missed out on the best that life had to offer by not having a meaningful relationship. I'd already thought the same thing myself—the day that Oliver and Sophie got married. I'd been wondering for weeks whether I was starting to show the first signs. Whether it might be the beginning of the end.' Josh's eyes darkened.

'And you chose that time to change how you looked. To cut your hair so that it swung loose and made me itch to run my fingers through it to see if it felt as soft as it looked. You got rid of your glasses so I could see clearly just how beautiful your eyes were. I'd controlled myself for so long and it was becoming unbearable.'

'And then there was Ben,' Toni said, almost to herself.

'Yes,' Josh agreed heavily. 'Then there was Ben. To remind me of why I'd made my plan in the first place. And why I had to stick to it.'

Toni closed her eyes against the pain. 'Last night?' she queried hoarsely. 'What was that all about?'

'I thought about what you said about Ben. About it being more cruel to leave someone not knowing whether their love was returned.' Josh sighed wistfully. 'And I wanted one perfect night for myself— with the woman I loved. I'm sorry, Toni.'

'I'm not.' Toni forced herself to hold Josh's gaze. 'And it's not over. I'm not going to let you leave.'

'I have to. I have to leave before my symptoms get any worse. This is my decision. It always has been ever since I decided, like Ben, not to get myself tested.'

The words hit Toni like a physical blow. 'You mean you don't know for sure?'

'I can recognise the symptoms.'

'Such as?' Toni's eyes narrowed. She was still trying to understand the implications of Josh's admission.

'The earliest ones are things like irritability and short-term memory loss. Having difficulty getting on with people.'

'We all have symptoms like that sometimes,' Toni protested. 'Perhaps you're just a difficult person, Josh.'

'Then there are involuntary movements. Accidents, like knocking glasses over and dropping things. An unsteady gait and lack of balance. I didn't have pins and needles in my foot today. I just started falling. It's been happening for days. I've got plenty of evidence, Toni. I know the list of symptoms like the back of my hand. I can quote you whole chapters of textbooks.'

Toni's exclamation was pithily derogatory. 'You sound like Mr Collins. Learn what the textbooks say and apply the symptoms. You can convince yourself of anything if you try hard enough.'

Josh jerked to his feet. 'Don't tell me what I'm trying to do. I *know* what I've got.'

'No you don't,' Toni shouted back. 'You just *think* you do. And you're too scared to find out the truth. What are you planning to do, Josh? Other than running away from St David's—and me. Are you planning to learn to fly, like Ben, and have an *accident*?'

'I don't know,' Josh groaned. 'It's something I'll have to deal with when the time comes.'

'No.' Toni scrambled to her feet. 'It's something *we'll* have to deal with. *If* the time comes.' Toni's eyes were very dark in her pale face. 'I'm part of this,

Josh, whether you like it or not. We might not be married but I love you and you're a part of my life I can't do without. For better or worse.'

Josh almost smiled. 'Till death us do part?'

'Exactly.' Toni's chin wobbled. 'You've already wasted years and years we could have had together, Josh. You're prepared to waste God knows how many years we could have. So what if it's not very long? We had one night, Josh. *One* night.' Toni didn't try to check the tears she felt gathering. 'And it was wonderful. Even one more night would be twice as wonderful.'

Josh's eyes were suspiciously bright as he moved to reach out for Toni. 'It's not that simple.' He folded her into his arms. 'They have a counselling process, neurological and psychological assessments. The blood test for the gene can take weeks.'

'So we'll have weeks together before we know for sure.' Toni tried to smile through her tears. 'That means we can both live in hope. And then we'll both know the truth.'

'And what then, Toni? What happens when the result comes?'

'Then we'll deal with it. Together.' Toni leaned back so she could look at Josh directly. 'It's not just *your* life we're talking about here, Josh Cooper. Don't you understand that?'

Josh drew her close again. His head rested against hers. His arms tightened and pulled Toni even closer. She could feel the beating of their hearts. She couldn't tell which pulse was hers and which belonged to Josh. But it was immaterial.

'Yes,' Josh whispered against her hair. 'I do understand. And you're right, Toni. I *was* too scared to find out the truth.'

'But you'll do it now?'

'No.' Josh was smiling. She could feel the movement of his lips. '*We'll* do it now.'

CHAPTER NINE

'JOSH isn't coming in today. He's not well.'

Toni's statement had all the effect of a bomb blast. Oliver, Sophie and Janet had gathered around the table in the staffroom at Toni's request. Only one patient waited in the reception area and that was old Paddy Smith. He would be close to the heater and probably sound asleep. Sandy was happy to be left in charge of the telephones and any more arrivals, though it was likely to be a very quiet day. Snow still lay thickly on the streets and the city had ground to a standstill. The St David's staff had all walked to work and it was nearly 10 a.m. by the time they'd all arrived. Now they sat, staring at Toni.

'He can't be sick.' Janet's stunned response reflected the others' expressions. 'Not sick enough to be off work. He hasn't missed a day in ten years.'

'He's missing this one,' Toni said calmly. 'He's asleep. At my house. I hope he stays asleep all day. Quite frankly, I think he's exhausted to the point of collapse.'

'He hasn't looked well for weeks.' Sophie nodded. 'You've said so yourself, Oliver. He's lost weight and he looks terrible.' Her eyes advertised her distress. 'It's not... Oh, God, it's not some kind of malignancy, is it?'

'Don't jump to conclusions.' Oliver's hand reached out for Sophie's but his intent gaze remained on Toni. 'What does Josh think the problem is?'

149

'He doesn't know for sure,' Toni said cautiously. 'He's noticed symptoms for some time. Short-term memory problems, irritability, lack of appetite and not sleeping.'

'Sounds like depression.' Janet said in amazement. 'But Josh is the last person I'd expect to be depressed.' Then she frowned. 'Maybe not. His approach to life is so full on. People can have mild manic depression and only ever exhibit the manic side, can't they?'

Oliver's nod was brief. His gaze returned to Toni. 'What about physical symptoms?'

'Remember when he said his foot went to sleep yesterday and he almost fell when he stood up?'

Oliver nodded again. He looked more serious than Toni ever remembered seeing him. 'He was covering up,' he said flatly. 'And it wasn't the first time.'

'Oh, God,' Sophie breathed. 'Not a brain tumour. Please!'

'For goodness' sake, Sophie,' Oliver chided her gently. 'It could be just a viral illness. Vestibulitis can have a dramatic effect on balance.'

Toni's head snapped back towards Oliver. 'What's vestibulitis?'

'An inflammation of the middle ear, involving the organs of balance,' Oliver explained. 'It usually manifests itself by unsteadiness, loss of balance and often by changes in hearing, like tinnitus. It can produce terrible dizziness or vertigo. It's usually caused by a virus.'

'He did have that rotten cold recently,' Janet contributed.

'But he's had the other symptoms for much longer,' Sophie pointed out. 'He's been like a bear with a sore head ever since we got back from our honeymoon.'

'They may mean nothing more than a reaction to stress. It's impossible to know without a full neurological examination and whatever other investigations are indicated.' Oliver's tone was crisp. 'Knowing Josh, he hasn't had any and he thinks he's made a correct diagnosis. Judging by the way you look, Toni and the fact that you've called us together, he thinks it's something serious. So come on. What is it that you're not telling us?'

Toni was silent for several seconds. She stared at her hands as she began to speak softly. 'Josh's mother had Huntington's disease. She died about twelve years ago. Josh made the choice not to have himself tested because he didn't want to live with such a death sentence hanging over him.' Toni's voice caught and she cleared her throat painfully. 'He wanted to make the most of life and he couldn't do that without at least having hope that he might be free of the disease.'

'He still might be,' Oliver said quietly. 'But now I understand.' He shook his head very slowly. 'That explains so much about Josh. God, the Ben Reynolds case must have put him through absolute hell.'

'What a terrible burden to carry alone.' Sophie had tears in her eyes.

'He's not alone,' Toni told them. 'Not any more. Josh has always avoided any meaningful relationships. He was determined never to have a wife or children who would suffer what his family went through. But there was one relationship he couldn't quite avoid.' Toni's smile was shaky. 'I love Josh. I always have. I've just discovered he feels the same way about me. I've told him that we'll see this through together—whatever the result.' She gazed at each of her colleagues in turn.

'Josh has agreed to go through the counselling and testing process. It's going to be a tough few weeks and we're going to need your support. That's why I called this meeting. To ask for your help.'

'We'll do anything we can.' Oliver had to clear his throat. Twice. 'Josh is the best friend I've ever had.' He smiled at Sophie. 'Until rather recently. I owe him a great deal.'

'He's like part of my family,' Janet said, her voice wobbling. 'He's the closest role model for a father the twins have ever had.'

Sophie was smiling at Toni. 'I'm just so glad you've found out how you feel about each other, Toni. God knows what he might have decided to do if you hadn't.'

'Mmm.' Toni's tone was noncommittal. 'I guess we'll never know.' She wasn't going to tell anyone about Josh's thoughts of escape. They'd stayed long enough last night to unpack all the boxes and put Josh's office to rights. Toni glanced deliberately at the clock. 'I think I've held things up for long enough. I'd better go and see how Sandy's coping at the front desk. Can you and Sophie cope with Josh's scheduled patients today, Oliver? There aren't too many and I doubt if they'll all make it. Nobody's going to be driving anywhere today.'

'Of course we'll cope.' Oliver nodded. 'Don't book anyone for me over lunch, though. I have a very important house call to make.'

Toni smiled gently. 'Thanks, Oliver. He might not be too happy that I've told you. He thought we should keep it to ourselves. But he'll appreciate your support. We both will.'

'How's Sandy coping with the job now?' Oliver queried.

'She's doing very well. Gets more on top of things every day.'

'Good. Then I think you should take the afternoon off. And any more time either of you need. We can get a locum in if necessary.'

Toni shook her head. 'I think we need to try and keep life as normal as possible. It's going to be hard enough, getting through the testing process.'

'What exactly is involved?' Sophie asked anxiously.

'It sounds like a big deal,' Toni replied. 'There's a genetic counselling session, a neurological examination and maybe a CT or MRI scan. Then there's psychological assessment and that's all before they even take the blood test. *Then* you have to wait for the results of the test and there's more counselling about the results.' Toni shook her head. 'I think we'll both need the distraction of doing our jobs. We'll fit whatever appointments we need in. I would like to go with Josh to everything, if he'll let me.'

The atmosphere at St David's the next morning was a little subdued but the large number of patients that came and went that day noticed nothing untoward. Maybe the staff members smiled at each other a little more often. Maybe they touched each other as they passed—a squeeze on an arm or a touch on a hand. And maybe Dr Cooper seemed to spend a little longer than usual in the office each time he entered, but the team at St David's had always been close. They were caring people and that was why the patients came. And kept coming in ever-increasing numbers.

Sometimes they came even when there was nothing wrong with them. Ruby Murdock had taken up power-walking and she used St David's as her turning point. The remnants of snow quickly vanished as the weather did an about-turn and decided it was really time for spring. Ruby was making the most of the sunshine and the fact that her daughter had returned and relieved her of the responsibility of three spotty grandchildren. Clutching her hand-weights, Ruby would propel her luminous pink or powder blue track-suit through the front door of St David's, pause for a quick chat with Toni, hopefully catch a word with Janet or Sophie, gulp a glass of water from the dispenser and then march out, beaming with the approval she had again received.

'She's an inspiration to a lot of people.' Janet said, grinning, after Ruby's third visit that week. 'I've had several enquiries about where to get the hand-weights.'

'What about the tracksuits?' Toni smiled, her hand stretching automatically towards the ringing telephone.

Janet laughed and shook her head. 'Nobody's asked where to get them.' She waited until Toni finished making the appointment the caller had requested and then lowered her voice. 'How did the visit to the genetic counsellor go yesterday?'

'Good.' Toni's smile was poignant. 'We got to discuss a lot of issues. Like the possibility of having children.'

'Is that an option?' Janet sounded hopeful.

Toni shook her head. 'Not yet. But it's another incentive to go through with the testing process.'

Not that any extra incentive was needed now. Toni and Josh were inseparable. They clung to the time they had together, as though trying to make up for a lost decade.

'We've got to get some sleep,' Toni protested, late that night. Very late.

'It's such a waste of time,' Josh growled. 'I'd rather talk…or…' His hand stroked Toni's breast gently. She curled against him, turning her back so that their bodies curved together comfortably. Josh's arm came over her body automatically. This was the way they slept now—when they did sleep.

'Toni?' Josh's voice floated in the darkness, minutes later.

'Mmm?'

'Do you want children?'

'Only if they're yours.'

'There's not much chance of that.'

Toni twisted in his arms a little. 'There could be. I've been thinking about what that counsellor told us. There's only a fifty per cent chance of a baby inheriting HD if you *do* have it yourself. And you can get a genetic test at an early stage of pregnancy. We could know for sure that a baby was clear before it was even born.'

'And if it wasn't?' Josh asked quietly.

Toni was silent. She could imagine the joy of having Josh's child growing within her. She couldn't begin to imagine having to contemplate a termination of that pregnancy. 'Is that why you're so careful about contraception, Josh?'

'Of course. And that's why I've only ever slept with very, very few women.'

Toni twisted even further. She tried to see Josh's face in the darkness. 'What? You've had screeds of women. I've lost count completely over the years. Your social life was a never-ending party. Only the guests changed.'

'And they changed quite often, as I'm sure you noticed.' She could hear the smile in Josh's words. 'It *was* a party, Toni. I needed the company so I didn't focus on myself. I wanted the sex but the risk was too great. There was no way I could pass this thing on to a child. And there was no way I wanted a woman dependent on me emotionally. Or me on her. Not that there was a big risk of that,' Josh added. 'As long as I kept away from anyone that reminded me of you.' He pulled Toni a little closer. 'Of course, I didn't realise that's what I *was* doing. Denial is a wonderful defence mechanism. You've turned my life inside out, Toni Marsh.'

'Would you rather I hadn't?'

Josh pressed his lips to her neck. 'God, no.' He propped himself up on his elbow, gazing down at Toni. She could just make out his features and the soft gleam of his eyes. 'I thought I'd experienced everything life had to offer. I had it all planned. I travelled to the world's greatest cities. I ate the best food, drank the best wine, spent time with as many beautiful women as I could find. I've been skiing, scuba diving, sky diving—even bungee jumping—and you know something?'

'What?'

'Any excitement I've ever found is nothing—nothing, compared to the feeling I have when I'm with you. When I'm inside you.' He bent to kiss her softly. 'It gives life a depth and meaning I had no idea even existed.'

'Oh, Josh.' Toni bit her lip. 'My world must be so dull compared to what you've been used to. I've never travelled or done anything very exciting. I've got my job and my house. My cats and my garden. And that's it.'

'Not quite.' Josh was moving in for another kiss. 'You've got me.'

'He's looking quite a bit better,' Sophie commented to Toni a few days later. 'He's a bit quieter than he used to be, though, and he still looks tired.'

'He hasn't been getting enough sleep.' Toni had to stifle her own yawn at the mention of sleep. Sophie peered at her and then grinned broadly.

'Oliver and I used to have that problem, too. Not any more. I go out like a light as soon as my head touches the pillow these days. I almost fell asleep between patients yesterday. I don't know what's wrong with me.' She looked longingly at the clock. 'I wish it was lunchtime. I'm starving.'

Toni had an odd expression on her face. 'You know those little plastic jars that Janet has in her cupboard? The ones with the pinks tops?'

'For urine specimens? Of course I do.'

'And you know the kit that comes in the blue box? The one with the little windows that the stripes turn up in?'

'The pregnancy tests?' Sophie's eyebrows shot up. 'Do you want one, Toni? Do you think you might be—?'

Toni was shaking her head sorrowfully. 'And I

thought it required a certain level of intelligence to qualify as a doctor. *I'm* not the one who's falling asleep all the time, Sophie Spencer. *I'm* not the one who's outrageously hungry all the time.'

Sophie chuckled. 'I'm sure it's just a side effect of being married. Especially on top of all the swotting I'm doing for my Primex exams. I've got the practicals coming up next month and I'm dead nervous.'

'You'll fly through.' Toni's smile faded quickly. 'Josh has his neurological examination coming up tomorrow. I'm dead nervous, too.'

Jack McMillan, in his early sixties, was a kindly, grey-haired neurologist. He was happy to include Toni in the consultation and drew her into his initial history-taking on frequent occasions.

'Tell me what you've noticed about Josh, Toni,' he encouraged her, having questioned Josh at length. 'Are the changes he's talking about obvious to you?'

'Some of them,' Toni admitted reluctantly.

'Such as?'

'I've noticed the tremor and the odd accident, like knocking over a glass of water. I guess when he lost his balance a couple of times it was most obvious.' Toni's expression was distressed but Jack McMillan merely nodded.

'That's only been very recently, hasn't it?'

'Yes. And it seems to have lessened in the last few days.'

Jack turned back to Josh. 'You had a viral illness just prior to noticing the lack of balance?'

'Yes.' Josh nodded. 'A nasty cold. That's cleared up completely now, though.'

The neurologist made a note and then glanced at

Toni. 'What about the other things? The irritability Josh has talked about. And the forgetfulness.'

Toni looked at Josh and smiled a little. 'Josh has always been inclined to be a bit irritable. Especially if he has a hangover.'

Jack McMillan smiled sympathetically. 'I know the feeling. Is that a frequent occurrence?'

'I'm not an alcoholic, Jack,' Josh cut in brusquely, 'if that's where you're heading.'

'Not at all.' The neurologist leaned back comfortably in his chair. 'Stress can lead to an increased alcohol intake which can produce symptoms that a lot of people would shrug off as a hangover. In your case, I suspect you wouldn't dismiss the symptoms so easily, which could lead to further stress. A vicious cycle.'

'I suppose I have been drinking a bit more just lately,' Josh admitted. 'I used to stick simply to wine, but not being able to get to sleep has led to a few nightcaps of whisky in the last few weeks.' He winked at Toni. 'Not to mention the odd splash of pink champagne.'

Jack McMillan's eyebrows rose but he made no comment. Instead, he stood up and opened his office door. 'Take a stroll down the corridor for me, Josh. Go as far as the nurses' station and then come back.' He watched Josh carefully as he complied. 'Now go half the distance with heel-toe walking.'

Toni was also watching Josh. He looked like a motorist asked to walk a straight line by a traffic policeman who suspected him of driving over the alcohol limit. She wondered what the neurologist was thinking as they all went back into the privacy of his office. Josh was asked to stand on one leg with his eyes open and then with them closed. He lost his balance quickly with his eyes shut. Toni chewed the inside of her cheek. Was that normal?

Jack McMillan spent some time testing Josh's vision. He got his patient to look straight at him, holding a ballpoint pen to one side, well out of visual range. He moved it slowly closer.

'Tell me as soon as you see the pen appear,' he instructed Josh. Then the pen came in from the other side, from above and below. Josh was asked to follow the pen's movements with each eye in turn after that, then Jack drew the curtains in the room, dimming the light to examine Josh's eyes using a bright pen torch and ophthalmoscope.

'I didn't think visual lesions were a major feature of Huntington's,' Josh complained finally.

'Just being thorough,' Jack told him calmly. 'Could you pull the curtains back for us, please, Toni?' He smiled at her. 'Let's get Josh to make a few faces.'

'He's good at that,' Toni said lightly. 'Especially when he's grumpy.'

Josh raised his eyebrows on request and looked surprised. He bared his teeth and looked fierce. He poked out his tongue and held it out. He puffed out his cheeks but couldn't hold the air against resistance. Toni giggled.

'Well, you try it,' Josh told her. He also smiled but Toni could see the tension in his eyes. This wasn't easy for Josh. He probably knew the reason each test was being performed. He was probably making as many mental notes as Jack McMillan was making written ones.

The examination went on. And on. Josh's hearing was tested. His head was held by the neurologist and rotated briskly from one side to the other. More strangely, Josh sat on the examination couch, his head again supported. Jack told Josh what he was about to do and asked him to relax. Then he tipped him quickly back so that his head hung down off the end of the couch, turned to one side. Jack repeated the odd test, turning his head to the other side, staring intently at Josh's eyes each time the manoeuvre was completed.

Finally Jack moved on to examine Josh's limbs, testing reflexes, muscle tone, strength and things Toni couldn't understand but which Josh was obviously familiar with. Like the sustained pressure pushing his kneecap towards his foot after Josh had relaxed his leg.

'I haven't noticed any knee clonus,' Josh told the neurologist.

'Bit difficult to test on yourself.' Jack smiled at Josh. 'But I'm sure you've tried all sorts of impractical methods of self-examination.'

Assessment of co-ordination gave Toni a few anxious moments. The tremor in Josh's hands seem to increase with each task. He had difficulty moving his finger back and forth from his nose to one of Jack's fingers rapidly. He was unable to hold a piece of paper between his fingers when asked to. Toni had to look away. She didn't want Josh to catch her gaze and recognise her fear.

The whole examination took well over an hour. Jack McMillan looked completely relaxed at the end. Josh looked exhausted.

'I can't find any definite indications of Huntington's,' he told Josh calmly.

Toni let out her breath, unaware until then that she'd been holding it.

'What about the problems with balance? And the tremor?' Josh asked seriously.

'I think you've had a dose of vestibulitis following your viral infection which would explain the loss of balance. I think you'll find it clears up completely in the next few days. I'll book you in for an MRI scan in the next day or two. We may as well be as thorough as possible.'

'And the tremor?'

'I wouldn't put too much significance on it, Josh. Or on the odd clumsy movement, like knocking over glasses. Stress can produce a number of symptoms. Sometimes just being aware of them exacerbates things. You didn't have a tremor at all when you were sitting in here initially. I know, because I was watching for it. It only appeared when I was looking at your hands and you began thinking about it.' Jack tapped the sheet of notes he'd taken.

'I'll get this written up and send you a copy. As I said, I can't find any evidence of symptoms that could definitely be attributed to Huntington's.' He glanced at Toni a little sharply as he heard her relieved sigh. 'I can't say you're not carrying the gene, of course, and the MRI scan may not show anything either. Only the genetic test can give you a definitive answer.'

'We understand that,' Josh nodded.

'You've had your genetic counselling session. I suppose you're well aware of the DNA pattern of tri-nucleotide repeats?'

Josh nodded again but Toni shook her head. 'I didn't understand that at all,' she confessed.

'Put simply, this repeat occurs in normal people

thirty times or less,' Jack told her. 'In Huntington's chorea it occurs more than thirty-six times, usually more than forty, and those people will develop the disease.' He turned back to Josh. 'Even if the test shows you are carrying the gene it can't predict when symptoms will begin or what course the disease might take in an individual case. It could start next year. It might not start until you're in your seventies.'

Josh nodded. 'That's why I'd rather not know. If I have got the gene I'd be expecting it any minute.'

'Isn't that what you've been doing already?'

'I thought I was showing early symptoms. Maybe I just created them.'

'Are you saying you'd rather not continue with the testing process at this stage?'

'I…' Josh caught Toni's dismayed expression. 'I don't know.'

Jack McMillan nodded slowly. 'This must be very difficult for you, Josh, and I understand completely. I see you have your psychological assessment interview booked for next week. That's standard before the blood test is taken. I expect you'll have some time to think about things and discuss them with Toni both before and after that assessment.' He stood up and held his hand out.

Josh took the offered handshake. 'Good luck,' the neurologist said warmly. 'I'll try and see you when you come in for the scan, but if I don't make it I'll ring you as soon as I've seen the results. Please, come and see me again if I can be of any help.'

Toni found the magnetic resonance imaging process frightening. She was allowed to sit in the technicians' room, walled off from Josh by thick glass. He lay on the narrow bed, his head held in position by cushioning. His body slid slowly into the huge machine. From where Toni was sitting she couldn't even see his feet. A technician leaned towards a microphone.

'OK in there, Josh?'

'I'm fine, thanks.'

'Right. Try and keep as still as possible. You'll hear some strange noises that will change in intensity at intervals. We'll run the first series of views now. It should take about five minutes.'

The noises *were* strange—vaguely ethnic, the rhythm and pitch changing every few minutes. Josh was spoken to between each series and it was a relief to Toni to hear his voice sounding quite relaxed. The images that appeared on the screens around her and the numerous plates which were taken and clipped to a viewing screen were astonishing. She could recognise the outlines of Josh's face quite clearly. She could also see inside his head. Not that she could interpret what she saw. A technician noticed her narrowed eyes as Toni peered at the screen.

'Nice to know he's got something in there, isn't it?' the technician joked.

Toni smiled but kept staring at the image. 'Can you see anything abnormal?'

'We couldn't comment even if we did,' she was told. 'That's up to Dr McMillan.'

Jack McMillan didn't make it to the imaging room before Josh and Toni left, but he rang St David's late that afternoon to tell Josh that the scan had been clear of any abnormalities.

'Another preliminary crossed off the list.' Toni smiled. 'We're getting there, Josh. Just the psychological assessment to go.'

'Hmm.' Josh gave Toni a guarded look. 'I'd rather go to that one by myself, if you don't mind.'

Toni did mind, but tried not to show it. Josh had every right to exclude her from such a personal interview.

'It's not that I want to shut you out,' Josh added. 'I don't even want to go myself. It strikes me as rather an intrusion. Too many people are poking around, trying to find out how I feel. Half the time I'm not even sure myself.'

'Maybe that's why they want you to talk about it. You haven't even said much to me, Josh. When you were talking to Dr McMillan last week, it sounded almost as if you'd changed your mind about having the test, but you haven't talked about it at all since then.'

'I'm sick of talking about it,' Josh said testily. 'I'm sick of thinking about it. I've spent the last twenty-five years thinking about it and making sure I didn't talk. Now I've got to start talking. Is it any wonder that I'm trying not to think about it between all these damned counselling sessions?'

'No. I'm sorry.' Toni backed away from Josh's anger. Then she changed her mind and went to him, wrapping her arms tightly around his tense body. He relaxed only slightly.

'Let's go home,' Toni suggested brightly. 'We don't have to talk. Or think. We'll find something to take our minds off anything stressful.'

'Such as?' Josh's arms finally moved to enclose Toni. He held her gently.

'Cooking?' Toni smiled. 'I still haven't given you that lesson.'

'I know how to make hash browns,' Josh reminded

her. 'And French toast. I could probably even manage the bacon and eggs.'

'But not the tomatoes.'

'No. I don't do tomatoes,' Josh agreed. He laughed and Toni felt his tension evaporate. 'I feel hungry all of a sudden.'

'Me, too.' Toni took hold of his hand. 'Let's go home.'

Josh's absence from St David's on Thursday morning was very noticeable. Everybody knew he had gone to his appointment with the psychologist but nobody wanted to broach the subject. Toni avoided the others when they took a break for morning tea by keeping busy in the office. Then she left Sandy in charge and took a walk down to the local shopping centre. Doing the banking and other messages had become one of Sandy's daily tasks but no one seemed surprised that Toni wanted a breath of fresh air.

It was fresh. She could smell the new growth as she took a slightly longer route that led near the bank of the Heathcote river. The grass on the banks needed cutting. The flower-like bracts on the elm trees clothed them in a delicately pale green. It was the sight of a line of ducklings, trying desperately to keep up with their mother, that brought Toni to a standstill. She watched the duck's purposeful march to the river and then saw each duckling leap bravely into the swiftly moving water.

A young woman with a toddler in a pushchair had also stopped to watch. The tiny child clapped her hands, her face alight with the joy of the scene. Toni had to blink back tears. Life was so precious. And joy could be such a fleeting thing. How much of either did she and Josh have left?

Toni bought a bunch of daffodils from the dairy. She arranged them in a small vase on her desk on her return to work and then took them into Josh's office, placing them on his desk where he couldn't fail to see them. He would know who had placed them there and he would understand the symbol of hope. Toni smiled a little shakily as she noticed the empty mugs. So much for that aspect of turning over a new leaf.

One of the mugs was resting on a textbook and had left a distinct ring on the cover. Toni rubbed at the mark until she realised it was just one of many. The book looked old and well used. It was a textbook on neurological disorders. Toni found herself sinking onto Josh's chair, her hands opening the book almost against her will.

The chapter on Huntington's disease was easy to find. The book had clearly been opened at that point many times. The lines burned into Toni's brain, the horror behind the stark print and clinical description almost unbearable.

'The illness is inexorably progressive,' she read. 'No treatment is available. Patients eventually lose physical and mental abilities to care for themselves. Walking becomes impossible, swallowing difficult and dementia profound. The majority of patients will require institutional care in the later stages of the illness.'

Toni slammed the book shut. There was no point in dwelling on a prognosis when the diagnosis hadn't even been confirmed. Even if Josh did carry the gene there was no way of knowing how long he had until the genuine symptoms manifested themselves. They could have years and years. Nobody knew what lay ahead. There were plenty of couples who began life together, expecting happiness only to have their lives torn apart by unexpected tragedy. That didn't mean they would have chosen to avoid the initial happiness.

But that, of course, was where the difference lay. For most couples, the possibility of disaster was so remote it was irrational to even consider it. The possibility for herself and Josh was far more real. A fifty per cent chance. A flip of a coin. Equal probability. Toni shook her head hard and pushed herself to her feet. This was the kind of mental path Josh must have trodden on countless occasions. It could easily destroy the quality of life still available.

No wonder Josh had hurled himself into living with such energy. And Toni could understand only too well now why he'd chosen to avoid the test. She could understand why Ben had pulled out before he'd finished the testing. Right at this moment she almost wished they hadn't started this process. She would have been happy to have kept the secret and simply joined Josh in making the most of every moment and still having the hope that it could go on for ever. But it was too late for that and Toni knew that living a fantasy would never work in the long term. If they did, in fact, have a long term.

Josh returned from his appointment with a cheerful grin for everybody. 'I'd like you all to know that I'm considered a completely stable individual. I'll have no more aspersions cast on my personality in future.'

'Want to bet?' Oliver smirked.

'Was it awful?' Sophie asked sympathetically.

'No worse than applying to the bank for a credit

rating,' Josh told her lightly. 'I passed, at any rate. The blood test is scheduled for tomorrow.'

There was a sudden silence. Toni's gaze went from Janet to Oliver to Sophie. She could see the significance reflected in all their faces. This was it. There would be no turning back once the results came through. No grounds for false hope.

'How long will you have to wait for the results?' It was Janet who voiced the question everybody wanted to ask.

'I'm not sure. It only takes a few days to do the test but it's a matter of where it falls in the queue. It could take weeks, but I hope it won't be too long.' Josh moved to disperse the impromptu staff meeting. 'This has interfered with all our lives too much already. Let's get back to work.'

Too long. And not long enough. A week ticked past. And then another. The stress of waiting began to tell. Toni left Sandy to cope alone in the office one afternoon and went in to see Josh between patients.

'I want to get married, Josh. Now.'

'I've got Tessa Dunlop with all four of her children in here any minute. Then I've got Helen Adams bringing her mother in. Goodness only knows what strife she's got into, juggling her medications around to suit herself this week. And I still haven't rung Mr Collins to discuss the implications of his exercise test.'

'That was negative, wasn't it?'

'Exactly. He's probably thinking of taking up marathon running and will want to discuss the possibility of some lung function tests. Anyway, as you can see,

I'm run off my feet. I really can't fit getting married in.' Josh's smile was cheerful. 'Sorry, love.'

'I didn't mean now, this minute,' Toni said seriously. 'I meant now, as soon as possible. Before we get the result.'

Josh shook his head. 'You can't be serious.'

'Yes, I can,' Toni said quietly. 'I'm very serious, Josh.'

'OK, I'll be serious, too.' Josh stood up and rested his hands on Toni's shoulders. 'There's only one thing that could persuade me to marry you, Toni Marsh, and that's a negative result on that test.'

'The result isn't going to change how I feel, Josh. That's why I want us to get married now. Before we know.'

'No,' Josh said angrily. 'Drop it, Toni.'

But Toni couldn't drop it. She had bottled up her emotions for too long. It wasn't humanly possible to keep up the cheerful pretence they'd both been maintaining so carefully.

'Please, Josh. It doesn't matter to me how long we've got. I love you. I want to give you the kind of commitment that marriage represents.'

Josh's face was grim. 'It might not matter to you how long we've got but it matters a hell of a lot to me. It's my *life* we're talking about here.'

'It's my life, too,' Toni shot back. 'That wasn't what I meant and you know it. I meant it doesn't matter in relation to getting married. We don't even know what the future holds, Josh.'

'We'll know soon enough,' Josh said woodenly.

'Some people get married even when they do know they haven't got long.' Toni was speaking rapidly. Desperately. 'Look at Bob and Diane Granger. They knew he had cancer when they got married. He'd only just got through the first lot of chemotherapy. They still had years together and they made the most of them. Diane told me once that it made their relationship more special because they—'

'I'm not Bob Granger,' Josh interrupted fiercely. 'I haven't got cancer. And I'm not going to marry you. Who would we invite? Oliver and Sophie? Janet? Would you want to see the pity they'd try to hide but not quite manage to? The knowledge that we're simply grasping at straws?'

'But we're *not*,' Toni said vehemently. 'Why can't you understand?'

'Why can't *you* understand?' Josh returned with quiet fury. 'Why are you pushing? I'm not ready to get married, Toni. Maybe I never will be.'

Toni's face whitened. 'Even if the result is negative?'

Josh's breath was expelled in an angry grunt. He turned away from Toni and took a very deep breath, obviously struggling for control. When he looked back his eyes held an apology but his mouth was set in a tight line.

'Perhaps being together so much is just adding to the stress. It's there between us all the time and it's making this all much harder.'

'I'm sorry.' Toni bit her lip, frightened by the distress she'd engendered. It was the last thing either of them needed.

'Maybe I should go back to my apartment for a few days.'

'No!' Toni whispered. 'I'm sorry, Josh. I won't mention it again. Let's forget I even brought the subject up.'

'It's not something we can forget. There's too much we're trying to avoid discussing right now. We're playing a game, Toni. It's not real.'

'My love for you is real.' Toni's voice cracked as tears threatened.

Josh smiled gently. 'So is mine. But we're hurting each other right now. I think we need a break.'

Toni swallowed painfully. 'If that's what you want, Josh.'

'Just for a little while,' Josh said softly. 'A few days.'

'Until we get the result?'

Josh nodded briefly. 'Just until we get the result.'

CHAPTER TEN

'HELLO!' Janet Muir sliced her hand briskly through the air just inches from Toni's nose. 'Any lights on in there?'

'Wh-what?' Toni blinked in surprise.

'You haven't heard a single word I've said, have you?' Janet accused her.

'No. Sorry, Jan. Tell me again.'

'It's not exactly important. I was just going through this medical suppliers' catalogue. I need a new uniform and I can't decide between this nice striped one with the kick pleats or this zip-front white smock with the shoulder epaulettes.'

Toni stared at the catalogue page. 'I like the stripes.'

'So do I. Now, blue and white, jade and white or burgundy and white?'

'No, thanks.' Toni reached for her mug and raised it, then she peered inside and put it down with a puzzled expression. 'Funny, I don't remember drinking it. Janet, did you drink my coffee?'

'I only drink tea, remember?' Janet closed the catalogue with a sigh. 'Are we on the same planet today, Toni?'

Toni smiled apologetically. 'I'm sorry.'

'You seem to be saying that a lot this morning.'

'I know. I faxed through three referral letters earlier. I sent the one that should have gone to the ENT specialist to a physiotherapist. And I sent the STD clinic referral to the ENT clinic. The receptionist thought it was hilarious. She rang and told me they don't usually deal with that end of the body but a bit of variety might be nice.'

'Did Ross come back for those samples you forgot to give him?'

'Yes, thank goodness. I'm useless at the moment. It's just as well Sandy's coming in for the afternoon. Things might start running a little more smoothly.'

Janet squeezed Toni's hand. 'It's OK. We all understand. This waiting must be absolute hell for you and Josh. It can't be much longer, surely?'

Toni took a deep breath. 'Josh got word two days ago that the test had been started. The results are due today.'

'How's Josh doing?'

'He's not saying much. Things are getting pretty tense.' Toni bit her lip. 'He went back to his apartment a few days ago. He said I was making the waiting unbearable by fussing over him too much.'

'It's hard on both of you. It must be so much worse for Josh, though.'

'I just want to support him.'

'Maybe he needs a bit of space to gather his own strength. It's a terrifying prospect. Whatever the result of that test, his life is never going to be the same.'

'Neither will mine,' Toni said slowly. 'I feel so confident sometimes—so hopeful of what our future *could* hold. Then I'm suddenly so depressed about it all. I can't bear to even think of the other side of the coin. It's like a roller-coaster.'

'Josh is on the same ride,' Janet reminded her.

'But we're in different cars,' Toni said sadly. 'We

should be together. It's—' She jumped visibly as the phone rang.

Janet gave her hand another squeeze. 'I'll get it.' She picked up the staffroom extension and then shook her head at Toni. 'If you can just hold on a tick,' she told the caller, 'I'll get the appointment book and see what we can do.' Janet put the call on hold. 'I'll go through to the office. Where's Josh?'

'On a house call. Louise Tyler called him to see her father. Sounds like he might have had a stroke.'

'Are you booking any patients for Josh this afternoon?'

'I haven't yet. I wasn't sure whether to or not.'

'Don't,' Janet advised. 'In fact, you should both take off when Sandy gets in. Go for a walk on a beach or something. Josh has a cellphone. We can always get the neurologist to call him on that.'

'That's not a bad idea. I'll see if I can persuade Josh.' Toni smiled as Janet dashed off to sort out the phone call. She rinsed both their mugs and made her way back to her office, passing Oliver on the way.

'I hope Sophie's OK,' Oliver muttered. 'Do you know she was so nervous this morning she lost her breakfast?'

'Really?' Toni was amazed. Being supportive was one thing, but... Then Toni smiled at Oliver as she connected. Josh's test wasn't the only important thing happening to a member of the St David's staff today. 'Sophie will be fine,' she assured Oliver. 'She'll fly through these practicals. When's the written exam?'

'Two weeks' time.'

'Great. We'll have to plan a party to celebrate the new partnership as soon as her accreditation is final.

A new partner. A new receptionist. St David's is booming.'

'Feels like it's about to explode.' Oliver grinned. 'All this tension. How are you and Josh coping?'

'We're hanging in there. Just.'

'Today's the day, isn't it?'

Toni nodded tersely. She could hear the telephone ringing again. 'Excuse me, Oliver, but I'd better get that.'

It was *the* call. Toni knew it was even before she answered it. The neurologist, Jack McMillan, had rung in person. What did that mean? Toni wondered desperately. Good news? Or not? The specialist's tone gave nothing away as he asked if he could be put through to Josh.

'I'm afraid not, Dr McMillan. He's out on a house call. Could I...could I take a message?' Toni asked tentatively.

'Not this time, Toni. Sorry.'

'No. Of course. It's just I...I...' Toni was stumbling over her words in her haste.

Jack McMillan broke in calmly, 'Has Josh got a mobile number?'

'Yes, of course. I should have thought of that.' Toni rattled off the digits. When she put the phone down she covered her mouth with her hand. She could visualise the consultant punching in the numbers. She could almost hear the slightly tinny ring of Josh's cellphone. She could feel her heart thumping against her ribs. They would be talking right now. How long would it take? Would Josh ring her back straight away or would he want to finish his house call and find somewhere more private?

The minutes ticked past. Toni made a start on opening the mail but then abandoned it. She stared blankly at the young man standing in front of the counter and he had to repeat his name twice. He gave Toni a strange look as he took a seat in the quiet waiting room. Janet came in to find a file. Oliver's patient came out to pay her account. Oliver came to take the young man through to his room. The minute hand on the clock continued its relentless movement.

And still Josh hadn't called.

Maybe Louise Tyler's father was seriously ill. Maybe the neurologist hadn't got through to him yet. Maybe he had asked Josh to go in to his office to discuss the result. Maybe Josh couldn't bear to tell her bad news.

Toni managed to last for an hour, until it was almost lunchtime and the empty waiting room and quiet phones made it impossible to ignore. She dialled Josh's mobile number. After three rings she got the modulated tones of the automated Telecom message.

'The mobile number you have dialled is currently switched off or outside the calling area. Please, try again later.'

Toni did try again later. And again. At 2 p.m. she ducked down to the shopping centre to do the banking. She should have sent Sandy but she simply had to escape briefly. Sandy smiled at her cheerfully when she returned.

'Josh rang a few minutes ago,' she said casually.

'Did he say where he was?' Toni glared at Sandy, who blinked in consternation.

'Yes. He's at the hospital. He's getting someone admitted. A Mr Taylor?'

'Tyler,' Toni snapped. 'And?'

Poor Sandy had no idea what she'd done wrong.

She was the only staff member who knew nothing about the drama going on in the lives of her colleagues. Now she looked flustered.

'And… and he said he had a few things to do and wouldn't be back this afternoon.'

'Oh, God!' Toni snatched up the phone and punched in the mobile number again. 'Oh, shut *up*!' she told the recorded voice. Fighting back tears of frustration, Toni caught sight of Sandy's expression. 'Oh, I'm sorry, Sandy,' she said contritely. 'I've been trying to get hold of Josh for hours, that's all. And I keep getting this bloody recording telling me to try again later. It's not your fault.'

'He said he'd talk to you later,' Sandy offered helpfully.

'Is that *exactly* what he said?' Toni swallowed painfully. 'Please, try and remember, Sandy. It might be important.'

'He said…um…' Sandy frowned in concentration. 'He said, "Tell Toni not to worry. I'll talk to her later." That's it!' Sandy's smile was triumphant. 'That's *exactly* what he said.'

Tell Toni not to worry.

Tell a fish not to swim.

Tell the moon not to rise and preside over the velvety blackness of the night sky, shining into Toni's garden with a cold brightness that was strong enough for the trees to cast perfect shadows. Toni could feel the grass crunching under her feet. It was going to be a very late frost for the year and it was going to be a hard one.

Toni shivered and looked back at the inviting glow of the house lights, but she didn't want to go inside.

She had spent too many hours waiting for the phone call that hadn't come. Waiting for the doorbell to announce the only visitor she wanted to see. The visitor that hadn't come.

Toni's despair gave way to anger around 3 a.m. How could he *do* this to her? How could anyone love someone and put them through this? Perhaps he didn't love her. Not the way she loved him, anyway. Perhaps the news had been good and now Josh knew he could have anyone he chose and not just someone who'd been prepared to stick with him through the bad bits. Maybe the news had been bad and Josh had packed up and left. Toni dismissed the thought with a stifled groan. Josh had promised they would see this through together. Even if she couldn't trust the strength of his love, Toni knew, absolutely, that she could trust that promise.

By 4 a.m., Toni was ready to slam the door in his face if he showed up. She was furious. Scared stiff and furious enough to throttle him. By 4.30 a.m. the cycle had returned to despair and Toni curled up in the corner of her couch, a cushion clutched against her as she sobbed uncontrollably.

The knock on the door came at 5.30 a.m. Toni stumbled as she reached for the handle. Exhaustion gave her voice the same impersonal qualities as a Telecom message.

'Hello, Josh. I thought it would be you.'

His face was unreadable. 'Get your coat, Toni. And some gloves and a hat. It's very cold and I want you to come with me.'

Toni didn't even ask where or why. Obediently, she followed the request. Without conscious thought she locked up the house and followed Josh to his car. He didn't say anything but the silence was oddly comforting. They were going somewhere to talk. There was no point in filling the silence before they'd reached the destination Josh had decided was appropriate. There was nothing else worth talking about.

Josh headed for the central city. It was still completely dark and the traffic almost nonexistent. Toni was too tired to wonder where they were going. She watched an ambulance ahead of them turn left to get to the hospital. Josh turned left a few blocks further up the one-way system, heading north. Then he drove over the judder bars that slowed vehicles entering the huge central city acreage of Hagley Park. The freezing temperature was making the waters of the Avon river steam. The trees were still dark silhouettes and the eerie vapour from the river curled beneath their trunks. A few hardy souls were already out jogging and a dog raced past Toni as Josh parked the car.

'Come on, we'll have to run.' Josh took Toni's hand as she climbed out. He turned away from the river and led her quickly towards one of the large areas of open grass. Toni could see a small truck parked in the centre of the field, with people moving around it. Then she saw the bright glow of flames.

'What is it, Josh? Where are we going?'

Josh slowed down and put an arm around Toni. 'You'll see. Be patient,' he said gently. 'You've waited a long time. A few minutes more isn't too much to ask, is it?' His eyes held an appeal that twisted Toni's heart. She gripped his hand more tightly as they began to run again.

As they came closer, Toni could see that the flames were from a burner. She could hear the roar as the burner was ignited at regular intervals. The air it was heating was rapidly inflating a hot-air balloon, a balloon that was attached to a large wicker basket, being steadied by two men. One of the men spotted their approach.

'Hi, there, Josh. Is this your lady?'

'Of course.' Josh smiled for the first time since he'd collected Toni.

'Hi, there. I'm Mack,' the man told Toni. 'I'm your pilot. We'll be another ten minutes or so if you want to stand over there and watch.'

The temperature dropped several more degrees as Toni and Josh stood, hand in hand, watching in awe as the giant balloon filled out and tilted majestically upright. The bright rainbow of colour was a glorious spectacle. The balloon had stripes of green, blue, canary yellow and orange. On a crimson section were huge stars in a luminous shade of sky blue. The air was absolutely still, the ground totally white. The massive old trees edging the park were sombre sentinels. The scene was unreal, so unreal that Toni didn't feel at all frightened when she was helped by Josh and Mack to climb into the basket. She welcomed the lurch as the anchor ropes were released, even though she knew that the ground was falling away beneath them.

The hint of red on the horizon deepened as the balloon cleared the trees. The river was still hidden beneath the blanket of vapour. An intense semi-circle of brilliant light peeped over the horizon and the whole sky lit up in a spectacular sunrise as the houses below got steadily smaller. The only sound was the occasional roar of the burner. Mack stood unobtrusively behind the backs of his passengers.

They were floating alone. Totally free. Together. It was a moment of pure magic. Toni gazed up at Josh.

'I love you,' she said quietly.

Josh's eyes echoed her words. 'I got the result, Toni. I needed a little time for it to sink in. To find the right way to tell you.'

'This is an amazing choice.' Toni smiled. 'I have no idea where we're going and I should be terrified but I'm not. I love it.'

'We can go anywhere we want, Toni. And you don't ever need to be terrified. Not when I'm with you.'

Toni took a deep breath. The painfully cold air scorched her lungs. 'You mean the result was good?'

'The result,' Josh said slowly, 'was perfect.'

'Negative?'

'Absolutely negative. I haven't got Huntington's. I can't pass the gene on to any children and...' Josh grinned crookedly. 'And I have no excuse not to ask you to marry me.'

'Yes,' Toni said happily.

'Yes—I've got an excuse?'

'Yes—I'll marry you.' Toni's gloved hands went around Josh's neck. The roar of the burner accompanied their kiss but Toni knew the heat she felt didn't come from that source.

'Mack?' Josh raised his head reluctantly and called over Toni's shoulder. 'Did you remember that champagne?'

'Coming right up, Doc.'

The outskirts of the city were left far below and behind them as they tasted the icy bubbles.

'Plastic glasses,' Toni said approvingly. 'But the champagne's not pink.'

'Some things are best kept private,' Josh murmured. His gaze held Toni's and she knew what he was really referring to—his plan to escape and possibly even follow Ben Reynolds's example.

'Absolutely,' she affirmed. They smiled at each other, their trust confirmed, their bond renewed.

'Josh? How are we going to get home?'

'The truck's following us, see?' Josh pointed at the road that divided the flat farmland below them. Toni peered cautiously over the side of the basket. 'We'll land before long and they'll take us back. We'll probably be in time for work.'

'I don't want to go to work,' Toni said. 'I feel like I haven't slept for weeks. It's almost too much to handle, having good news. I was so keyed up to deal with something else.'

'You and me both. I had the oddest reaction initially. Almost disappointment. I couldn't believe that I could have been so wrong, could have wasted so much of my life. Then I felt ashamed of myself. And angry. I arranged this balloon ride days ago and then I actually forgot about it. I spent the whole time since Jack rang me trying to get a grip on things. That's why I rushed you off. I thought we were going to be late.'

'You're exhausted, too.' Toni stroked Josh's cheek with her gloved hand. 'You haven't been well and you've had all this stress on top of it. You need a good long rest.'

'My thoughts exactly.' Josh looked over the edge of the basket. 'We're coming down.'

'Oh, no! I was just getting used to it. I don't think I want my feet back on the ground just yet.'

'We'll do something about that,' Josh promised.

'Why don't we plan on an extended honeymoon? Six weeks or so. We'll go somewhere exotic. Somewhere peaceful. We can both have some rest and recuperation before we plant our feet back in reality.'

'Where would we go?'

'Nowhere too exciting. I don't want any distractions.' Josh leaned closer to Toni. 'We're not getting any younger. Do you think we should plan on getting pregnant on our honeymoon?'

'Absolutely.' Toni's eyes shone. 'Let's find a desert island. Palm trees and sandy beaches and weather that's too hot to worry about clothes.'

'Let's find lots of desert islands,' Josh agreed. 'We'll cruise the Pacific or the Caribbean and try them all.'

'When shall we go?'

'As soon as possible. Shall we get married here or on one of those islands?'

'We'll have to do it here,' Toni said with a smile, 'or the others would be too disappointed.' She gasped. 'They don't know! Oliver and Sophie and Janet. They don't know about your result.'

'*Our* result,' Josh corrected her. They were looking at each other as the basket touched down with a bump. Josh caught Toni in his arms to balance her but the basket dragged along the ground without tipping.

'How's that?' Mack shouted proudly. 'Perfect landing!'

Josh and Toni were still gazing at each other. Now they smiled and spoke together in total agreement.

'Perfect!'

MILLS & BOON®

Makes any time special™

Mills & Boon publish 29 new titles every month. Select from...

Modern Romance™   Tender Romance™

Sensual Romance™

Medical Romance™ Historical Romance™

MAT2

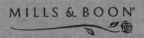

MILLS & BOON®

Medical Romance™

THE BEST MAN by Helen Shelton

Bachelor Doctors

As best man to David, surgeon Josh Allard is brought back together with Paige, David's ex-girlfriend. The long ignored spark between them is still there but is the timing right?

THE TRUTH ABOUT CHARLOTTE by Lilian Darcy

Lucy Beckett had nursed Dr Malcolm Lambert's wife during the last stages of her life and had not seen him for six years. Now they are working together in A&E and their respective daughters are best friends. But can they resolve their past?

ON THE RIGHT TRACK by Rebecca Lang

Dr Clay Sotheby seems to have everything going for him. But having met nurse Sophie Dunhill, he starts to question his priorities as he discovers he can't put her out of his mind...

On sale 3rd November 2000

0010/03b

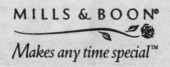

4 FREE

books and a surprise gift!

We would like to take this opportunity to thank you for reading this Mills & Boon® book by offering you the chance to take FOUR more specially selected titles from the Medical Romance™ series absolutely FREE! We're also making this offer to introduce you to the benefits of the Reader Service™—

- ★ FREE home delivery
- ★ FREE gifts and competitions
- ★ FREE monthly Newsletter
- ★ Exclusive Reader Service discounts
- ★ Books available before they're in the shops

Accepting these FREE books and gift places you under no obligation to buy, you may cancel at any time, even after receiving your free shipment. Simply complete your details below and return the entire page to the address below. *You don't even need a stamp!*

YES! Please send me 4 free Medical Romance books and a surprise gift. I understand that unless you hear from me, I will receive 6 superb new titles every month for just £2.40 each, postage and packing free. I am under no obligation to purchase any books and may cancel my subscription at any time. The free books and gift will be mine to keep in any case.

M0ZEA

Ms/Mrs/Miss/Mr ....Initials.................................
                                                        BLOCK CAPITALS PLEASE

Surname ....

Address ....

....

....Postcode...............................

Send this whole page to:
UK: FREEPOST CN81, Croydon, CR9 3WZ
EIRE: PO Box 4546, Kilcock, County Kildare (stamp required)

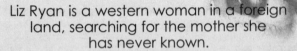